ABOUT THE AUTHOR

Rachel Tsoumbakos is a stay home mother of two.

Her main passions are writing, reading and organic gardening. Rachel lives with her husband, two kids, three cats and seven chickens in suburban Melbourne, Australia.

While she has several articles published through mainstream magazines, she has also written extensively for *The Inquisitr*.

Over the years, Rachel has been interested in many aspects of history. When studying a Library Studies diploma, she discovered just how much she enjoyed researching and has since used these skills in several of her novels.

However, it was her work with *The Inquisitr* that brought her into the world of the Vikings and she has spent several years delving into the sagas of this culture as well as the history of the Viking Age.

FIND RACHEL ONLINE:

Facebook:
http://www.facebook.com/rtsoumbakos
Twitter:
http://twitter.com/#!/mrszoomby
Blog:
http://racheltsoumbakos.wordpress.com
Newsletter:
bit.ly/RachelNL

Vikings: The Truth About Aslaug and Ragnar

RACHEL TSOUMBAKOS

VIKINGS: THE TRUTH ABOUT ASLAUG AND RAGNAR

Rachel Tsoumbakos

COPYRIGHT © 2018 by Rachel Tsoumbakos

MYRDDIN PUBLISHING GROUP

ALL RIGHTS RESERVED

Cover art: © Nejron | Dreamstime.com
Cover design: © Rachel Tsoumbakos
Time breaks designed using the Angerthas free font
Edited by Alison DeLuca

unique electronic & print books

For Mum.

CONTENTS

We fought with *swords*. Now I find for certain that we are drawn along by *fate*.

Who can evade the decrees of *destiny*?

~"The Death Song of Ragnar Lodbrog," also known as the *Krákumál.* Translated by Thomas Percy in *Five Pieces of Runic Poetry Translated from the Islandic Language* (1763)

Introduction

The Vikings and the sagas about them have always been a fascinating subject. They were a vicious breed, fierce, yet steeped in tradition and their own moral code. While many Vikings have captured the imagination of those who read about their feats, it seems the tales of Ragnar Lodbrok and his sons are some of the most recognised today thanks to History's television series, *Vikings*. Along with Ragnar, the fascination continues through to his romantic partners. While many are captivated by the story of Ragnar and Lagertha, many find the relationship between him and his other wife, Aslaug, somewhat harder to digest thanks to her portrayal in the television series. However, as you will discover, Aslaug has a rich and exciting story and her love for Ragnar was just as mesmerising as that of Ragnar and Lagertha.

The Truth about Aslaug and Ragnar will delve into the stories that involve this power couple and attempt to unravel the truth about Ragnar Lodbrok and wife, Aslaug, who was considered a volva, or wise woman, in her own right. Along with this discovery, I will be exploring other versions of Ragnar and Aslaug's romance as viewed by historical documentation, as well as present day perceptions of this famous Viking couple.

The Truth about Aslaug and Ragnar is also different to previous accounts of their tale. This book is both a historical discovery and a fictional adventure. Many books delving into the history of the Vikings are historical, non-fiction events that aim to uncover the historical truth behind Ragnar and Aslaug according to the evidence. While my book will also include this sort of information, for those of you who prefer to learn about history by reading about it as if the people involved were characters in a novel, this book will also pique your interest. Using the historical information obtained from the first part of this book, I will capture Ragnar and Aslaug's story in a fictional account of their romance as well as Aslaug's earlier, more informative years prior to their relationship.

When deciding to write a fictional version of Ragnar and Aslaug's story, the first thing I needed to decide was in what tone and language I wrote the novel.

Unfortunately, many of Aslaug's sagas have not been readily translated into English, so it has been hard to get a direct version of some of her stories. However, thanks to a modern translation by Ben Waggoner, I was able to get a fairly descriptive version of her tales. As a result of this, my novelisation of Aslaug's and Ragnar story will be using the version of English we all speak today with a slightly old English flavour to make it seem like you are reading a text from long ago, such as is displayed in translations such as Ben Waggoner's.

This will not be without challenges however. After all, the characters will speak in a manner that is current English, however, at times, they will resort to phrases common for the original time frame in order to remind the reader this story happened hundreds of years ago. It will certainly be a balancing act between reminding the reader of the period and making the story jump out from the pages because the content is familiar.

As well as choosing the language in this novel, I also had to decide on the common names to use throughout this book. While Ragnar's name remains fairly consistent (especially his first name), others, not so much. Aslaug is now only known by her usual name, but also takes on a couple of pseudonyms in her tales.

Along with this, the ever-present problem of alternative spellings of names is ever present. For example, Aslaug has several children to Ragnar. However, the names of these children can differ between tellings. As well as this, sometimes Aslaug's children can be attributed, not only to differing names, but to a different mother, Thora, who was also a wife of Ragnar. When researching Aslaug's sagas, it makes more sense to use the names from the *Saga of Ragnar Lodbrok*. Yet, because of the differing names, and links to mothers, it becomes a challenge as to what to name Aslaug and Ragnar's children. So, what happens here? After much consideration, especially in relation to the next point, I have decided to use names in relation to the sagas involved. Therefore, in this book, Aslaug's sons will bear the names given in the majority of the sagas pertaining to Aslaug.

Something else to consider while researching and writing this—and subsequent books in the series—is the fact that, between sagas, events can change quite significantly. The timeframe for Lagertha's relationship with Ragnar as it occurs in the *Gesta Danorum* indicates many discrepancies in relation to Ragnar's relationships with his other wives. It is the general assumption, based on the sagas involving Ragnar Lodbrok, that Thora was Ragnar's first wife and Aslaug was his second.

However, the *Gesta Danorum* has a very strange timeline that makes it difficult to place many of the events in a logical order, especially when compared with other stories involving Ragnar, Thora and Aslaug. For example, in order to make the timeline of Ragnar and Lagertha to work in the first book in this series, *Vikings: The Truth about Lagertha and Ragnar*, I have had to manipulate some storylines. In particular, placing Lagertha as the second wife of Ragnar, after Aslaug in order to make Sigurd old enough to go to battle in the fictional retelling. However, if you look at the sagas involving Ragnar, Thora and Aslaug, this timeline does not make sense as there is, potentially, a very questionable relationship between Aslaug and one of Thora's sons.

As a result, each book in this series will be able to be read as a standalone book. All characters will be set in, basically, the same timeframe as each other. Some of these stories will certainly overlap, and, where possible, I have tried to maintain a consistent story between each novel. However, if there is conflicting stories, I will always choose to maintain the integrity of the stories being used for each particular book. Therefore, this series will take on the oral tradition seen with the Vikings sagas in that each story can change with each telling.

While each book is considered a standalone, there is also some parts of each story that become integral over different novels, so can also be read as a series. Take, for example, Aslaug's story. In *Vikings: The Truth About Lagertha and Ragnar*, Aslaug's story is touched on thanks to the timeline of Lagertha's involvement with Ragnar. However, there are also clues left behind that suggest there is more of Aslaug's story to tell. These will definitely be explored further only by reading this book.

If you are partial to a factual look into history, this book is for you. Various Viking sources along with other historical sources will be evaluated in an attempt to piece together the true story about Ragnar and Aslaug.

If you are a lover of historical fiction, this novel is for you as well. *Vikings: The Truth about Aslaug and Ragnar* will also turn historical research into a fictional account of Ragnar and Aslaug's love story.

So, settle back and enjoy the ride.

ⒼLOSSARY

When you first start out in Norse mythology and the Viking sagas, there are a few words you may come across that are unclear in definition. Included below are all the terms from this novel that may need an explanation.

Asgard: The place where the Norse gods reside. It is connected to the earth by a rainbow bridge called Bitfrost.

Folkvangr: (Also known as Fólkvangr) A mythical field ruled by Freya. She takes half of those slain in battle here while the other half go to Odin in Valhalla.

Freya: (Also known as Freyja, Freyia, and Freja) A goddess who is most often associated with associated with love, sex, beauty, fertility, gold, war, and death.

Freyr: (Also known as Frey, or Yngvi-Freyr) Not to be confused with the goddess called Freya, who is his sister, Freyr is said to be the god of sacral kingship, virility and prosperity, and fair weather. He is one of the Vanir, the son of the sea god, Njord. Considered to be an ancestor of one of the Swedish royal houses.

Knarr: A type of Viking merchant ship.

Kraka: A female name meaning raven.

Njord: (Also known as Njörðr) This god is most often associated with the all things pertaining to the ocean, as well as wealth, and crop fertility. The father of Freya and Freyr.

Odin: (Also known as the Allfather, Óðinn, Woden) Odin

is the head of all the gods in Norse Mythology. He is akin to Zeus from Greek mythology and Jupiter in Roman mythology as all are considered the top of their pantheons.
Shield maidens: (Also known as shieldmaidens) Viking women who chose to fight in battles alongside men. They are also mentioned in some old Germanic stories. It is possible shield maidens are a human representation of the valkyries.
Skald: Someone known to write poetry about heroic deeds and important events. They could be compared to a bard or minstrel as the skald would compose and perform their poetry for entertainment. Although it is unclear whether skalds played musical instruments while performing like a bard did.
Thor: This god is the mighty hammer-wielding god of thunder and lightning. He is also tasked with protecting mankind.
Valhalla: A hall located within Asgard that is said to house all of the warriors who have died during battle or as the result of other heroic deeds.
Valkyries: Mythical women who were sent during battle to select who lived and died. Those chosen by the valkyries would go to Valhalla or Fólkvangr after they died.
Vanir: A group of gods that is usually associated with fertility, wisdom, nature, magic, and the ability to see the future.
Volsung Clan: (Also known as Völsung, Völsunga, Vǫlsungr, and Vǫlsungar) Volsung was the head of the ill-fated Volsung clan, a famous Nordic family, which included Sigurd, Aslaug's father.
Volva: (Also known as völva, vǫlur, vala;spákona,

fjǫlkunnig) A female shaman, seer or wise woman. In Old Norse, the word volva translates into "wand carrier" or "carrier of a magic staff."

Wine-leek: According to the sagas, a wine-leek could sustain a person for a very long time, even if they ate very little. The translation for this word could also mean wine-onion or wine-garlic.

ART ONE

THE TRUTH ABOUT ASLAUG AND RAGNAR

(A historically accurate retelling of Aslaug and Ragnar's saga)

PLEASE NOTE: In some cases, fictional names have been used where the real names of characters could not be established.

ℙROLOGUE

THE WOODS WERE DARK AS SHE ENTERED. IT was still early, after all, and the sun was only just breaking light. Her hands reached out, touching the trees as she passed, grounding her with their mere presence.

Aslaug was determined as she walked. The frigid cold of early morning did not chill her. The damp earth, still frosted over, did not freeze her. It was her vision that terrified her and nothing else entered her mind as she made her way through the forest.

She remembered her dream, oh, how she remembered it. The sight of Ragnar's agonised face bit into her memory and consumed everything else, no matter how hard she pushed the images away. In the end, there was nothing left to do but remember it; those moments when she had foreseen her husband's imminent death. She choked back a sob as she thought about it. Losing Ragnar was more than she could ever bear, and she had endured so much already in her lifetime.

Flashes of pain wracked her body as she remembered the departure of the longship and the arrogant way in which Ragnar had claimed he would visit England and defeat those there. These were the same people that others of their kind had not been able to conquer in all their years of raiding. The vision had revealed Ragnar would leave the shores of Norway with only two boats instead of a fleet. It was such a preposterous notion.

Aslaug stopped. Leaning forward, she sagged against a tree, its rough bark biting into her flesh, yet she felt no pain. How could she, since the prospect of losing Ragnar was all-encompassing.

She bit at her lip, tasting the tang of blood and being relieved at that fact. It meant she was alive. And while her heart still beat, she would do everything within her power to make sure her vision did not eventuate.

While her people believed their fates were in the hands of the gods, Aslaug was not so sure. Her visions over the years had tempered her ingrained belief that their lives were fated, never to be changed over the course of time. Aslaug had seen things in visions, things she did not doubt would come to pass. However, she had worked hard and sometimes helped to change the course of destiny.

She pulled herself back from the tree, stood upright, still for a moment, her head looking skyward as the sky started to lighten. Perhaps her visions were merely warnings of what could happen if she didn't alter her course of action. She wondered if this was the truth. It would match up with what everyone said about the gods after all. Aslaug moved on, each step was slow and deliberate, as she thought. Either way, it did not matter what she thought about the gods and destiny. If the gods were showing her these things, she needed to take action. Whether it was to change events, or to keep on the path the gods had put her on, the outcome would be the same.

Aslaug stopped then, at the thought of losing Ragnar. She sobbed; a loud, ugly sound that startled the birds from the treetops around her. Doubling over, Aslaug reached down and grasped at the leafy ground. Clawing the debris, she grabbed handfuls of the loam and threw it high into the air, her anger forced out of her in a sharp scream. The dirt and leaves rained down on her as she clung to her sides and cried alone there in the forest, far away from anyone she cared about.

Gathering herself, as the dirt stopped falling, she swallowed her grief down. She had work to do. Ragnar's very life depended on it. Staggering to her knees, she wobbled a moment before drawing herself up.

Each torturous step in front of the other, the weight of tragic love heavy upon her, she plodded through the forest, searching. Regardless of the drain of potentially losing the man she loved, she fought through the pain, the anguish, and set her mind to the task of gathering ingredients for a vital piece of magic. It was a long time before Aslaug returned home, her arms weighted down with a multitude of plants and other materials that could be woven together.

Emotionally spent and physically exhausted, she dropped the items inside the door of her house before gathering her children to her. Aslaug hugged them fiercely, as if they were the ones she was about to lose, instead of her husband. She touched their hair and smelled their necks before sitting down with her newly gathered items. She watched her children as she worked, they didn't know it, but they helped to channel her energies while she wove Ragnar a silk vest.

A vest that she hoped would help him cheat his foolish, prideful death.

CHAPTER 1:

𝕴N THE BEGINNING

ASLAUG'S STORY STARTED BEFORE SHE WAS even born. Her parents, Sigurd the famous dragon-slayer and his wife, Brynhildr, herself a shield maiden, had many tales spun about them.

Sigurd, having fashioned a magical sword out of his father's shattered one, took on the dragon, Fafnir, at the advice of his foster father, Regin. With the help of Odin himself, Sigurd devised a plan that would down Fafnir. Afterwards, drinking the blood of the dragon, it was said that Sigurd could then understand the language of all the words across the lands. However, the birds then revealed to Sigurd that his foster father was being corrupted by a dangerous and magical ring. At their behest, Sigurd killed Regin.

It was after this event that Sigurd met Brynhildr. Aslaug's mother had sided against Odin in a battle previously and had, therefore, been shunned to a mortal life. Holed up in a castle, Sigurd fought his way through and cut off her armour, thus claiming the shield maiden as his own, using the aforementioned cursed ring to claim her.

Sigurd had fallen instantly in love as Brynhildr did with him. However much she loved him though, she also knew that their love was not fated to stand the test of time as a result of the ring Sigurd gave her. She told him as such, but he would never believe her until the day came when, at the court of Heimir, Sigurd was given the Ale of Forgetfulness. This caused him to turn away from Brynhildr and marry another woman who went by the name of Gudrun.

Brynhildr, in her anger and despair, also wed someone else, a man called Gunnar. After a while, Brynhildr and Sigurd's new wife, Gudrun, argued over who had the better husband. This quarrelling had dire consequences as the plot to have Sigurd forget all about Brynhildr is finally revealed. Gunnar, worried Brynhildr might return to her first husband, killed Sigurd. Brynhildr, devastated when she found out, threw herself onto Sigurd's funeral pyre and willed herself to die rather than stay trapped in her mortal shell any longer.

It was said that Brynhildr and Sigurd's marriage was filled with great passion, but Aslaug could not attest to this as she was only three years of age when they both perished and she was placed into the care of Sigurd's trusted friend, Heimir.

And this is where Aslaug's story truly began, trapped ever in the shadow of her parents doomed love. As a result of her parents peril, Aslaug also wound up in a physical bind as Heimir hid her away from the world in the giant case of his harp. They were then forced to take on the role of beggars to maintain their secret identities rather than have Aslaug meet the same fate as her parents.

CHAPTER 2:

HEIMIR

HE GAZED DOWN AT THE CHILD, PERFECT IN every way, a reminder of the mess of Sigurd and Brynhild's love affair. Heimir was despondent. For all that had gone wrong in Sigurd's relationship with the shield maiden, it wasn't the child's fault. In fact, this child, Aslaug, was the single thing that had gone right in the relationship. And that meant that he must do everything within his power to make sure this small babe had a better chance in life than her famous parents.

Heimir was unsure just how much of her mother's otherworldly powers she had inherited, but that didn't matter for the moment. With all the upheaval and jealously surrounding her heritage, Aslaug was starting life at a disadvantage. Heimir had to find a way to ensure her parent's woes did not follow her around forever. Whether Aslaug grew up to be powerful as a result of her valkyrie blood would have no consequence if Heimir failed to protect her in the here and now.

For many days Heimir locked himself away in his room, surrounded only by those guards he trusted implicitly. Even still, he worried. Everyone was capable of deceit, he knew this for certain as a result of all Sigurd's troubles. If his own wife could be tricked into forgetting about him, if Sigurd could be murdered because of a jealous desire for power, then even Heimir's own guards could be considered traitorous in the current climate.

He paced the room from sun up until sundown, only stopping briefly to eat. Even then, the food he consumed was from stock he had collected and tested himself first. No one had died eating his goods. He paused as he raised the food to his lips. A deep breath. Then another. Finally, he gulped the first bite down, letting no time for regret to sneak into his resolve. The barley bread stuck to the roof of his mouth, his saliva dried with fear. He chewed, once, twice, and then swallowed a quick gulp of mead to wash it back. The food stuck in his throat, like the regret of not being able to protect Sigurd, and he gulped some mead to wash it down.

He had to find a way to protect Aslaug and himself. Looking around the room that he had made his own personal prison, he saw nothing but finery. He bed was laden with grey wolves' furs and finely spun woollens in vibrant shades. He had many fine items of jewellery and personal items that would fetch him many riches.

Yet, what would it be worth to him if he were dead? He reached out and touched a brooch. It had belonged to his father, the insignia indicating their family line and standing. But what could it do for him now, as he stood in his prison?

Absolutely nothing.

Heimir threw the item across the room.

If they died, would his and Aslaug's social standing really matter?

Perhaps he should give this all up? Could he live the life of a beggar in order to keep Aslaug safe? Heimir wasn't sure. All his life he had only known the luxury of high standing. His slaves were just faceless figures who did his bidding. No, losing himself and Aslaug within the anonymity of the lower classes would be too much for Heimir to undertake.

He paced some more.

Yet, wherever his mind took him, he always looped back to the fact that he was identifiable. Everyone knew who she was, therefore they would know who this new child within his possession was. At the end of the day, it was Aslaug he had to keep safe at any cost.

And, so it came to pass that Heimir decided he would have to humble himself. He would learn how to live like a peasant. In fact, he would live lower than a peasant would. He would take his expensive clothing and discard it. He would don rags and take Aslaug with him and he would renounce his title and everything that went with it.

Even though he felt sick at the thought of roughing it in a way he had never even imagined, let alone wanted, there was a settling within his bones. It was as if he was free of the constraints he never knew he was fettered with and he saw his world with a new light. They would have to live in a small house filled with herbs and onions hanging from the rafters, paid for in sweat instead of coin. Heimir saw the selfishness he had always possessed and the arrogance with which he had ruled. A humble awe was enveloping him as he was alerted to the struggles of those he had never even considered.

Heimir gazed down at Aslaug as she slept at his feet. This tiny child, this baby who he never knew he wanted or needed had made him a new person. Already he was amazed at how something so small could alter his world so dramatically. And yet, he had never even knew his world needed changing, or that he would relish the change so much.

ONCE HEIMIR SET HIS mind to giving up his worldly goods and title, he faced another challenge. How would he smuggle Aslaug out of here? He had arrived without being sighted by anyone and was able to hide Aslaug easily. However, even though Aslaug had remained quiet since he locked them away, there had been a few narrow escapes. It seemed one guard was not as trusted an ally as he first thought. While he didn't know who it was, another guard had suggested there were rumours going around the marketplace about how Heimir now had a girl child in his possession. A couple of people had approached to find out the truth and Heimir was getting nervous that these whispers might travel further than just this town.

Although, perhaps he was worrying about nothing. Brynhildr was more than a mere human so perhaps Aslaug was too. If valkyrie blood did flow through her veins then the gods would recognise her importance and make sure she would not be found out. Although, that hadn't protected her mother.

Heimir stared down at the small child, only three years old, yet with ever-knowing eyes that bore into him with a sadness and the knowledge that he was going to protect her. A fierce need rose up in Heimir. He would protect her. He could protect Aslaug. He had to, without even knowing why. But the why wasn't important anymore. As he broke their gaze, he sighted his old harp in one corner of the room. An idea began to form.

Kneeling down, he spoke to Aslaug. "Can you be quiet while I am gone, child?"

Aslaug nodded.

Standing, he strode from the room and set about getting a harp made as quickly as possible. It would be a giant harp, like no one had ever seen before. It would be large enough to conceal those worldly goods he could use to trade without identifying him. It would also be large enough to hide a growing girl.

CHAPTER 3:

$\mathfrak{A}$SLAUG

"HEIMIR, CAN WE STOP HERE?" ASLAUG WAS tired of the journey. Heimir was able to see everything as they travelled, yet Aslaug was always confined to the harp case. She was sick of the movement beneath her as the rhythm of Heimir's pace jostled her glorified cage. Perpetual progression, yet everything she could see around her never changed.

"We can't yet," came the muffled reply. He spoke softer than normal, so Aslaug knew there were people about. However, he wasn't quiet enough to indicate they were in a great crowd. She sighed. Closing her eyes, she settled back once more. The movement lulled her, tempered her irritation slightly.

Eventually, Heimir spoke. "There is a waterfall up ahead, would you like to stop there?" His voice was more confident this time. Obviously, no one was present.

"Oh, could we?" Aslaug sat up, although the effort was becoming harder now she had grown so much. The harp case grew ever smaller by the day. Aslaug's world was shrinking in a way that was tangible to her as she watched the walls and nestled into the decreasing pile of clothes and items they could sell.

THE SUN WAS BRIGHT as the case was opened. It

wasn't until her eyes adjusted that she knew if the day was sunny or if it was just her time confined to darkness that hurt her eyes.

Aslaug held her hands up over her eyes like a roof to protect them while her pupils adjusted. Yes, it was sunny today. The warmth coated her skin with its gentle, nourishing kiss.

She darted across the small clearing. Nervous energy that had been bottled up for days now burst from her as she tore around the field. Clapping her hands together, she giggled with glee. Heimir laughed at her and she smiled broadly at him.

"You need to bathe," he said as he handed her some dried fish.

Aslaug took it and sat down at his feet. She chewed at the food and looked at her dirty feet. Yes, she certainly needed to clean herself. She could also smell the stale, pungent tang of her cramped confines. There was nothing they could do to remove that odour other than pack the harp case with herbs before they left on their journey again.

"That is the last of the fish, Aslaug," Heimir conceded. "While you bathe, I will see if I can find some more wine-leeks."

Aslaug screwed up her nose at the mention of wine-leeks. They were her staple diet and the reason for the heavy aroma inside her confines. They could sustain her and Heimir for great lengths of time regardless of how few they ate.

"I know you don't like the idea," Heimir admitted. "However, I cannot keep buying food as we travel. You can see already how many items I have had to use for trade. Your harp case will be empty before you have grown up and moved on with the way we are trading.

Aslaug sighed. She knew he was right. It didn't mean she had to like it though. She stood then, ready to strip down and relieve the rid herself of all the travelling dirt she had accumulated since the last time she had been able to wash.

The river was icy as she entered, yet Aslaug didn't mind. She dove under the water and felt her long hair stream through the water as it tugged her head back slightly. It was her crowning glory, Heimir always told her. Even at the age of ten, it hung down past her waist. While she travelled inside the harp, Aslaug braided it and wound it around her head to stop it from tangling and knotting. Now that she was free of her confines, she had unwound her hair and brushed it out until it shone in the sunlight. It was one of the few things that entertained her while they travelled. Aslaug would endlessly unwind it and braided it in complicated ways to keep herself occupied. She let the water pull the kinks free and her hair flattened out in the cool water.

After Aslaug finished scrubbing her body, she floated away from the noise of the waterfall. She gazed at the sky, squinting against the heat of the day

It seemed that her entire life had been nothing more than the insides of Heimir's harp case, broken only occasionally by moments like these when she was free to witness the world around her. Aslaug couldn't remember her life before Heimir had adopted her, although he had told her all the amazing stories about her parents. To be honest, Aslaug didn't care much for Sigurd and Brynhildr. While Heimir waxed on about how amazing the couple were and the gallant things her father had done, Aslaug resented more than admired them.

Her father had lived a full life, mingling with the gods and fighting dragons with his magical sword called Gram. Brynhildr was supposed to be like a goddess, according to Heimir, being a valkyrie. But all Aslaug thought was that her mother was an idiot for siding against Odin and ending up suffering as a human when the Allfather found out.

In fact, if Aslaug was to be entirely honest with herself, the anger she felt at her parents went beyond resentment at the fact they had lived full lives before dying. Aslaug was furious that her parents had lived so hard and loved so much that they had expired rather than stay here with her. Warm tears seeped from Aslaug's eyes and into the cold river as she floated in the comfort of the water.

Aslaug tried to imagine what her life would be like if her parents hadn't been selfish enough to die while she was so young. If they had loved her as much as they had loved each other. A sob tore from her throat and Aslaug sunk into the water. Reaching out, she felt the solid graze of rocks and she pulled herself into a seated position. She wrapped her arms around her middle and allowed herself the luxury of crying for a moment.

She tried to remember their faces. A flash of blonde hair and a stern smile was all she could picture of Sigurd. Then, darker hair braided tight: her mother, Brynhildr. The same two images were all she could ever conjure up. Aslaug was never certain these were actual memories or if they were just wishful thinking after all the stories Heimir had told her. Either way, it did not matter, she figured as her parents were gone and her life was nothing more than a moving trap.

"Let me play the harp for you, Aslaug." Heimir's voice startled her and Aslaug swiped away her tears angrily.

"That would be lovely, Heimir," she replied.

The music started slowly. The melody strummed out on the delicate strings and flowed over her, softening her taunt muscles. As she emerged from her makeshift bath, Aslaug allowed the music to spirit her away.

CHAPTER 4:

HEIMIR

THE DAY WAS WARM, SO MUCH WARMER THAN Heimir was used to further north in the reaches of Norway he was used to. He moped his brow and paused a moment. It was only the middle of the day but he felt like his body was turning to liquid as he carried Aslaug in his harp case.

"Are we stopping?" Aslaug's voice was as quiet as the movement of grass on a windy day, yet Heimir heard her, accustomed as he was to her quiet ways now.

"Not yet, Aslaug," Heimir replied before setting off again. "I think I see a farm ahead though. Perhaps we will stop there for a while. It is so hot today."

"Please, Heimir, that would be wonderful." Her voice rose with anticipation, tugging at Heimir's heart.

Besides the few times Heimir had caught her crying, it seemed to him that Aslaug had completely accepted her new life. Heimir had struggled in those first few months on the road. Many times he turned, ready to ask someone else to do tasks for him. It had taken months for the surprise of them travelling alone to truly sink in and Heimir had finally stopped expecting others to do his bidding. After that, it was worse as he could concentrate entirely on how much he missed Sigurd and his foster daughter, Brynhildr. At times, he had gasped as he walked, causing Aslaug to startle and ask if he was alright. While he had been great friends with Sigurd, it was Brynhildr he missed the most. Every time he gazed down on their daughter, Heimir had seen Brynhildr staring back at him.

The road they followed now was rocky and Heimir stumbled. Each step seemed to bring him grief as he remembered his past, his gilded life and those precious people. More important than all the finery in his harp case now, he remembered those he wished he could trade his life for to bring them back.

ᚴ

THE FARM SEEMED ABANDONED as Heimir approached. The day was beginning to lengthen into late afternoon. Already warmth was turning to the chill of night. A shadow seemed to cover him as his trepidation elevated. He couldn't work out why he felt anxious as he approached. Besides the fact the buildings appeared rundown and dilapidated, there was nothing to suggest there was danger hiding nearby. Perhaps it was just the sudden drop in temperature as evening began to creep in that created his feeling of unease.

Yet, Heimir trusted his instincts. There had been times on the road, over the years, when Heimir had not let Aslaug out of the harp case even though they appeared to be alone and secluded because he had felt the uneasy snake of cold fear sliding down his spine. Most of those times, his feeling had proven correct and people had appeared when they shouldn't have.

But now, Heimir doubted his gut feeling. The closer he got to the farm, the more he realised it was likely just a farm.

Everything seemed to be as it should. Plus, Heimir could request to stay the night in an out building rather than with the farm owners. That way, Aslaug would be safe.

Even as he had this thought, he shivered.

"Are we there yet, Heimir?"

"Shh!" He was abrupt in his reply and Aslaug instantly silenced herself. The farm loomed in front of him now and evening was encroaching as he called out. "Is there anyone there?"

Silence. He called out again.

"Hello!" The voice was distant and Heimir turned in the direction of it. A large, ugly woman approached.

"I am after a place to stay tonight," Heimir explained when the woman finally reached him, panting as she leaned forward to catch her breath. The fetid stench of her hot breath washed over Heimir and he tried not to gag. "I do not need much, just a roof over my head. Do you have an unused stable or outhouse I could shelter beneath?"

The woman stood, looking Heimir up and down. Her gaze paused on the harp placed on the ground next to him. He stood in front of it, hoping the fringe of fine material that he had just noticed peeking out at the base had not caught her attention.

"My husband is not here at the moment, but I am able to speak on his behalf. We surely do have a place for you to stay tonight."

"That would be wonderful," Heimir said as he rubbed his hands together against the encroaching cold. "But first, could I please warm my hands against a fire? The evening chill is already approaching."

"Of course, why don't you step inside then," the woman replied as she opened the door to the farm and stepped inside.

"I am called Heimir. What is your name?" Heimir asked as he followed her through the door.

"I am Grima. My husband's name is Aki. Our farm here is called Spangareid," the woman replied. She turned to look at Heimir. "Please tell me, why are you travelling with such a great harp? Are you a musician or a skald?"

"No, I am not unfortunately," Heimir replied, lowering his head." I am a mere beggar, looking for a place to shelter my head for a night, away from the harsh weather for a change. This harp is the very last thing I own."

They didn't talk much after that. Heimir set his harp down and watched as the woman tended to the embers of the fire. Finally, flames rose up and he stepped forward, cupping his hands over the welcome heat. Quickly, he ducked his hands back into the sleeves of his coat when he realised he was wearing an expensive ring. Glancing over, he saw Grima busying herself with stirring a pot over the coals.

"Perhaps you could show me where I will be staying tonight?" Heimir asked, uncomfortable in the silence. The feeling of unease had never left him since he'd arrived here and Heimir was looking forward to spending some time apart from this woman already.

Grima lead Heimir outside, talking as she went. "You will probably better off sleeping out here than in the main house with Aki and I. We both speak very loudly when together and I am afraid we might keep you awake all night."

Heimir laughed. "I am sure you would keep me from my slumber. I am used to the sounds of the forest now and not of people."

"I imagine so," Grima replied as she pushed open the door to an old barley barn. " You can sleep in here tonight. I hope you enjoy your rest. I must leave you now though as I have much work to catch up on before my husband gets home."

Heimir nodded at Grima as she exited the barn. He watched as she made her way back to the main house and only released Aslaug from her confines once Grima was inside the farmhouse.

"Aslaug, it is safe now," he uttered as he unhinged the case.

The girl stepped out cautiously and looked around. Her eyes would adjust quickly in the dim surrounds of the barn. Yet, still she stood there, as if waiting for something, or assessing the situation in front of them.

"I don't like that woman, Heimir," Aslaug finally said.

"Nor do I, sweet child. But, it doesn't matter any I suppose as we will only be here a night and then moving on. A roof over our heads is still shelter, regardless of whether we like the source or not.

"I suppose," Aslaug said with a nod. "I would watch yourself around her though."

Heimir had always wondered if Aslaug had the sight thanks to her valkyrie blood. Now a shiver of dread ran down his core.

"Do you know something I don't, Aslaug?"

"I'm not sure." She was hesitant and she gazed off into the distance, as if she were seeing something not even present in front of them. "I just wish it were morning already and we were gone from this place."

"Me too."

They settled down to sleep after that, the fog of dread sinking down on top of them both like a deadly weight.

CHAPTER 5:

ⒼRIMA

"WOMAN! WHAT HAVE YOU BEEN DOING ALL day?" Aki was gruff as he sunk down in front of the fire. Grima rushed forward, already anticipating her husband's foul mood.

"Relax, Aki," she said as she handed him a cup of warm ale. "I have had a visitor today."

"So, a visitor is more important than your husband, is he?" Aki swallowed back the ale and belched. Grima refilled his cup and hopped he would mellow with the alcohol.

"No, not at all dear husband. But I think this guest will bring us good fortune."

Aki starred at her. She could see it in his eyes, the disbelief that was always there. Their lives had been hard, yet Grima was always optimistic. It had been some time since Aki had played along with her schemes to help their burden.

"I seriously doubt it. After all these years, you haven't managed to lighten our load at all. This time will be no different, you'll see."

"Please, don't be angry," she insisted, pouring Aki another tall cup of ale. "This man will certainly change our destiny. All I need is one small task from you and then we will never have to work again."

Aki rolled his eyes and looked away. Already Grima could see he was past caring about the conversation. "She sat down and reached for one of his hands, determined that he would listen to her.

"A man, Heimir, came to Spangareid earlier today and asked for lodgings for the night. He calls himself a beggar, but I know better. What beggar carries a harp case with him after all?"

"Maybe he keeps his wares inside," Aki suggested.

"If so, those wares are more expensive than he likes to let on." Aki looked at her now, for the first time in the conversation he was interested in what she had to say. "I bet that case is filled with costly items, judging by the fine fringe of clothing I saw peeking out from it. The man also wears an exquisite ring on his hand. I suspect he was once a great champion and is now destitute for one reason or another. Yet, he still carries all his finery with him, hidden away in that case. All you need to do is kill him and we will be richer than anyone ever suspected of us."

"Kill him?" Aki looked shocked. "I don't think it's right to take the life of one of the few people who visit here."

Grima pursed her lips, rage starting to flare at the edges of her mind. "You are the very reason we have amounted to nothing, Aki! Everything is always too hard for you. This man is old, beaten down. How hard would it be to kill him at the end of such a long life? It wouldn't be a betrayal, but a mercy. If you are not careful, maybe I will put you aside and take this old man as my own. He was very eager to talk to me today, I could tell there was interest there. You have two choices, Aki. Either you kill him and we live well, or you let him live and I will leave you."

Aki stared at her, long and hard. She could see the conflict there. He had always been a soft man, underneath the angry and gruff exterior. Grima waited patiently while her husband mulled the idea over in his head. It wouldn't be long now. She poured him another ale.

CHAPTER 6:

Aki

ALTHOUGH THE AXE WAS ALREADY SHARP, Aki still held its head to the whetstone. Aki needed the distraction, he needed to sober up from all the ale Grima had plied him with up to this point.

"Surely the axe is sharp enough now?" Grima's voice was harsh, similar in sound to the noise the whet stone made as he ran it against the metal of the axe. Aki shuddered as he closed his eyes.

"Yes, I suppose it is," he replied. It was time.

Aki stood, dropped the whetstone onto the bench next to him and edged his way towards the barn. It was dark, the night closing in around him like a gaggle of gossiping women. Aki turned, Grima stood at the edge of the farmhouse, holding the doorframe for support. Aki wished he could change places with her, he needed the support of the building more than she did.

Each step felt like slogging through heavy mud as he approached the old barley barn. Not a sound could be heard from inside. In fact, not a sound beyond his rough breathing could be heard at all around him. It was like the night was waiting, watching, judging him.

The giant barn door yawned open. He paused, swallowing hard. Glancing back, he was met by the sight of Grima shooing him forward. Aki wanted to run back and use the axe on her. He wanted to lop off her head rather than of the innocent man inside the barn whose only fault was choosing a place such as theirs to spend the night.

Aki turned. There was no choice. While he didn't really want to kill the man, he would hate for Grima to leave him either. For all her faults, Aki loved her well and couldn't imagine how he would cope living all alone after their long time together. Their life had been hard and now it seemed like it was finally time to relax.

As he approached the barn, he slowed his pace, testing each footfall to make sure he didn't step on a branch and awaken Heimir. The dark night was illuminated by a full moon and it was just light enough to see into the barn. Two unfamiliar shapes greeted him. One stood upright and Heimir shied at first, thinking Heimir was awake and standing to greet him. Aki stopped, clutching at his chest, his heart beating a jumpy staccato within his chest.

It was only the harp case, nothing more.

Searching the darkened barn once more, Aki rested his sight on the other foreign lump within. Heimir's body. He lay, stretched out, on the barn floor amongst the dust. Aki approached, his steps inching slowly, infinitesimally, towards the deed his wife had set him.

Soon he was close enough. Aki raised the axe, paused, then brought it down swiftly, the weight of the implement making him more decisive than he actually felt.

The hit was brutal, hitting Heimir at an angle that caused more blunt force trauma than axe wound. The axe had rotated slightly as Aki swung and the blade hit more on its side than its sharpened edge. The man woke with a start, a roaring scream issuing from his mouth before he had even worked out what was going on. Aki could see it in Heimir's eyes, the fear of the unknown blending with the fear of knowledge. Heimir knew as he woke that he would die, Aki read it clearly in his face.

Even though Heimir appeared to know he was to die, it didn't make his struggle any less. Aki watched as the man threw himself about the space, gagging and clutching at the wound. Heimir stomped his feet so vehemently that the ground shook. Aki jumped back out of the way, but stumbled and fell with the movement of the earth beneath him. As he scrambled back out of the way, Heimir rocked backwards and forwards, his feet staggering one way and then the next. He lurched and screamed, the sound reverberating inside Aki's head until he squeezed his fists to his ears in an attempt to block out the sound.

Abruptly, Heimir threw himself against a pillar within the barn. It seemed the whole building shook with the impact of the man. Aki scuttled back even more, out of the barn, for fear the whole building would collapse on him. And still Heimir roared out as his death throes grew in intensity.

In fact, by the time Heimir dropped to the ground, finally silent and dead, the barn had collapsed. When Aki stood, looking around, he also noticed their farmhouse had succumbed too. Still, the earth shook beneath him. As Grima approached, she swayed along with the movement and Aki saw trees doing the same.

When Grima reached Aki, he reached out and clasped her to him, thankful they were both still alive. They stood together, entwined, waiting for the world to still.

"It is done, Aki," Grima said when everything was silent and settled once more. "I am so proud of you, my husband."

Aki smiled down at his wife, the woman he loved, yet despised just as much.

"Let's open this harp case then, shall we?"

CHAPTER 7:

Aki

THE HARP CASE HAD TO BE BROKEN INTO, AS Aki and Grima were not skilled in such arts as lock picking.

"Use the axe, Aki," Grima prompted while Aki grabbed its handle and swung with more determination than he had at Heimir. The case cracked with the wound and the image of blood flowing free flashed briefly before Aki's eyes. He remembered Heimir's initial scream. Aki concentrated on swinging the axe once more.

"Did you hear that?" Grima asked as Aki swung. The blow was stilted as a result. Nevertheless, it was enough to force the hinge of the case to splinter and open. Aki dropped the axe and he and Grima pried the case open.

"What in Midgard is this?" Grima stepped back as she spoke. Aki, however, remained rooted to the spot, for from the harp case, a girl appeared. She was thin and beautiful as she uncoiled herself from the tight confines. Her face was white and pinched, like she had witnessed unspeakable horrors.

"Is that a girl?" Aki was horrified. Finally, he glanced over at the old man they had killed. He wept openly. "I am so sorry."

"Shut up!" Grima roared.

But Aki was done with pandering to his wife. He was shocked and horrified. While an old beggar was not worth worrying about, it now appeared the victim had a child. Aki had killed someone who was dear to this beautiful girl. Aki's anger overcame his sorrow and he could feel a fury building towards his wife.

The young girl just stood there, directing her gaze evenly between Grima, Aki, and Heimir.

"What have we done!" The words hissed out from between his teeth, his face running red with seething anger. "This poor girl is now an orphan thanks to your horrendous plan. I knew this would happen. I knew if we killed someone who had sought shelter under our roof, the repercussions would be dire."

Aki paced, his hands fisted tightly and his face a thunderstorm of fear and rage.

"It's not true," Grima consoled him.

"Oh, but it is! Can't you see? We have taken the life of someone who trusted us. We killed someone innocent. The gods are repaying our deed accordingly."

The girl never moved, never uttered a single word as Aki paced in the dusty straw. He was unnerved by it all, as if the gods were showing their decision through the child.

"This girl is a gift, Aki. Don't you see it?" Aki was confused. He stopped pacing and starred at his wife, wondering if she had finally gone completely mad. "We can use her to help us on the farm. Neither of us is getting any younger, are we? She will be a great help to us. We can pretend she is our own child."

Aki stared at the girl. She gazed back at him, like she could see inside his head and read his very thoughts. Aki blinked, breaking their tenuous connection, and turned back to his wife.

"No one will believe a girl as beautiful as this one came

about as a result of us two. Look at us, we are horribly ugly." Aki said the words to wound his wife but she didn't hesitate before answering him.

"People around here do not know me as a young woman, they will think I was once attractive like this child. They will talk about how a hard life has made me ugly and wish this child to not have the same fate."

Instead, her words wounded him. Aki had no reply and simply walked away from the whole mess. He made his way, step, by agonising step, back to where the farmhouse had once stood and laid down in its rubble to sleep.

I

THE MORNING BROUGHT ABOUT its own level of torture, Aki discovered. When he finally arose from the numbing joy of sleep, he remembered the night before and felt his stomach instantly tighten. He had hoped it had all been a dream, a horrible nightmare that would dissipate when he awoke.

Instead, he got to witness Grim cutting away the girl child's stunning hair. Not content with the fact hair will always grow back; she prepared tar and rubbed it over the girl's scalp.

"What on earth are you doing, Grima?" Aki asked as he approached.

"I will hide her beauty as much as I can, Aki," she replied as she put a hood over the girl's head. "She does not appear to speak, so I have named her Kraka, after my mother."

"She would be so proud," Aki replied. He felt the ale and brown bread rise in his throat. It was intolerable to think he'd have to confront what he had done in the girl's fearful eyes—every hour of every day.

So, from that day forth, and for many years afterwards, Aslaug became known as Kraka.

CHAPTER 8:

℞AGNAR

"THORA IS DEAD."

Ragnar gasped. Stepping back, he gaped at the messenger. He tried to speak, to yell at the boy to leave him alone before Ragnar killed him for being the bringer of such horrendous news.

The boy could obviously see the intent in Ragnar's face. He backed away, turning when he reached the door and fleeing for his life. Ragnar wanted to run after him, to grab him by his thin neck and squeeze the life right out of him.

It would not bring back Thora.

He slumped, his whole body suddenly weak from the grief and realisation that he would never lay with his wife again, never talk to her, or to hear her sweet voice.

Ragnar sat on the ground, remaining still, yet tears streamed down his face. He remembered back, all the way, to the beginning, to when Thora had a lindworm problem and Ragnar had been able to fix it.

He had been so young then—only fifteen—but always ready for adventure, when he heard about Thora's plight. Her father, Herrud, an earl in Gautland, loved his daughter and often remarked that she was the most beautiful woman in his lands. No man who had laid eyes on Thora could disagree.

As a result of this, Herrud spoiled his daughter, giving her gifts and praising her highly whenever he could. Having raised Thora to expect gifts every day from him, he found, as she got older, the task was becoming more difficult.

However, one day he had happened upon a little heather snake. As soon as he laid eyes on the delicate creature, he knew Thora would love it.

And, love it she had. Too much, in fact. The heather snake flourished as she fed it and cherished it. Every day she would place a small piece of gold underneath the snake. Over time, it grew too big for the box where it lived. After their marriage, Ragnar asked Thora to tell him the story of the strange creature. She complied, describing what happened to the massive creature.

The snake would loop itself around the box, inside Thora's bower. However, eventually it grew so much that even her bower was too small to contain it. Finally, she had allowed the animal—who had changed from a lowly heather snake into the much more treacherous lindworm by now—to wrap itself around her home, protecting her from the outside world.

When the animal grew so big as to require an ox every day for nourishment, Herrud had finally put his foot down. He decreed that anyone who could kill the lindworm could marry his daughter.

Ragnar had been victorious. He smiled at the memory of defeating the animal. He had donned thick, shaggy pants that were covered in tar in order to protect himself from the dangerous animal. And, when the earl had seen Ragnar's attire, he had instantly given him the nickname, hairy breeches. And so it had stuck, and now everyone called him Ragnar Lodbrok rather than Ragnar Siggurdsson.

Wiping his eyes, Ragnar remembered the birth of their fine sons, Eirek and Agnar. They were such big lads now, tall and strong, just like Ragnar had been at their age. They were handsome too, but dark like Thora. Whenever they entered a new town, women would flock to their sides, even before people were aware they were the sons of Ragnar Lodbrok. They made him proud. But, they had made their mother prouder. Not a day passed when Thora wouldn't admire her boys, giving praise for their actions, or commenting on how successful they were with women.

Ragnar gasped with anguish.

How was he supposed to go on without Thora?

"How?" He roared the word out, as if the empty room could answer for him.

Instead, Eirek rushed into the room. Ragnar looked up, his own wet eyes meeting Eirek's damp ones. "You have heard the news then?"

"Yes, Father." Eirek crumpled down next to his father. Ragnar reached out, one strong arm enveloped his son and drew him in for a fierce bear hug. "How are I and Agnar supposed to go on without our mother?"

Ragnar shook his head. "I don't know."

But, he knew what he would do, personally. Ragnar would go raiding. Since he had married Thora, he settled down into married life and ruled over his lands. However, now Thora wasn't there to stabilise him, and to make sure he did the correct and kingly things, he would resort back to his younger antics.

He would raid, and attack, and kill things. It would not stop the pain he felt in his heart, but it would help to quell it, to squash it down under the thrill of attack and plunder.

CHAPTER 9:

℞AGNAR

HE GAZED OUT OVER THE EXPANSE OF water. Land had been sighted that morning and Ragnar was eager to alight onto Norwegian soil. He had been true to his promise on the day he heard the news about Thora. He had left the very next morning with a fleet of ships. Ragnar sailed far and wide, taking what he could, killing those who opposed him. Some of those he killed had been insignificant, the lowly commoners of foreign lands. Others were more substantial. In fact, on this trip, Ragnar had even been able to kill an English king, a man named Hame. He smiled when he thought of that death. His grief and anger made him a very formidable person now. But, it meant nothing to Ragnar. Each night, as he lay down to sleep, the blood of battle usually still on him, the rusty tang faded, replaced only by the longing to smell the scent of Thora's sweet skin one more time.

It took him many months of travel to discover that raiding did not make the hollow feeling of new grief subside. And that is why he was now approaching Norway. Not to conquer or annihilate, but to visit with kin and strengthen ties with friends. Having paid a visit to Gautland, he visited the place where Thora had been given her final send off to Folkvangr. He then travelled around the coast, towards Norway. Here he planned to rest awhile, to gather his thoughts and decide what he would do with the rest of his life. Norway was as good a place as any other for this devastating task, he decided. He was also planning to travel to Sweden at some point, to visit with the king called Eystein.

"Tonight we will hunker down under the stars on dry land," Ragnar called out to his crew. There was a brief cheer at the anticipation of finding a town that stocked women and wine.

However, there had been no town when they landed. Instead, the shoreline stretched out as barren as one of those English women who refused a husband in favour of the Christian god. Ragnar had searched one way, and then the other for signs of a settlement, but there had been none. His crew were disappointed until someone pointed out that there was plenty of mead on board. As they set up to stay the night, someone fetched the mead and soon Ragnar's men were content.

Ragnar took a skin of ale and travelled up the beach a little way. The noise of his men dulled somewhat and he lay down in the sand, looking to the stars as the world spun around him.

"I have had too much to drink." There was no one about, but Ragnar was making his confession to the gods anyway. "Please Odin, give me love again. I am only young and I cannot imagine being without someone like my dear Thora—" He choked then. Saying Thora's name did it to him every time. He cried briefly, an ugly sob or two and then he chugged some more ale. Wiping his eyes, Ragnar decided he was done with talking to the gods. He stood, taking another swig from his ale skin and walked back to the fray.

"What are your plans, Ragnar?" Rolf asked as Ragnar returned.

"I have no idea, Rolf. What do you think we should do?"

"Hmmm," Rolf ran his fingers through his beard, as if he was giving the idea some genuine thought. "We should search for a town on the morrow, I think. I need a woman."

Everyone laughed and cheered at that comment. Ragnar rolled his eyes instead.

"Is that all you think about, Rolf?"

"Of course," Rolf retorted instantly.

"Well, then, a town we must find. But, first, we need to

stock up a little. Tomorrow we bake bread instead." A groan erupted at Ragnar's words.

HIS CREW MAY NOT have liked the idea of baking over breeding, but, in the morning, his men set about to make bread.

"Oi, Ragnar!" Olaf called out. "There is a farm up ahead. We can go there to make bread, rather than try and make it here on the beach."

"What a good idea, Olaf," Ragnar replied. "I will see you when you return then."

And so Ragnar's men set off to the farm which was called Spangareid.

CHAPTER 10:

𝕲RIMA

"HELLO?"

Grima stepped out from her house when she heard the stranger call out. She still had a half-eaten barley cake in her grasp as she greeted the group of men. "Can I help you?"

"Are you the lady of the house?"

She took another bite from the cake and nodded. "I am Grima.

"My name is Olaf, and I am here on behalf of Ragnar Lodbrok. We need to bake some bread and this farm is the perfect place to do it."

"Of course," replied Grima. She could see by their clothing that they were important people, so she didn't doubt there were here on behalf of Ragnar.

"Perhaps you could help us?" Olaf asked.

Grima shook her head. "I am old and my hands are not what they used to be." She held her gnarled fingers up in demonstration. The men nodded at her. "I have a daughter though, she is young and able. Kraka is out in the fields with our livestock now, but when she returns, I will insist she help you. She is unruly though, so I can only try."

Kraka had been a gift when they first found her, all those years ago inside the harp case, even if Aki had insisted she was a curse as a result of their lacking hospitality. They had put her to work at the farm and immediately their lives had become easier. Kraka did not speak much and, at the time, seemed not to know she could object to their instruction.

Over the years, though, as Kraka grew, she began to revolt against Grima. Aki, on the other hand, was tender towards their foster daughter, and he allowed her to get away with far too much. Therefore, Aki seemed impervious to Kraka's bad behaviour.

At the start, Grima had resented the girl for her beauty. Regardless, she was still happy to have the child help around the farm. Now, she found she could not stand the sight of the girl even though Grima had found ways to keep hidden the girl's beauty. In fact, Kraka's insolence had taken first place in Grima's quest to make the girl's life miserable. In so far that when Aki had insisted Kraka be able to grow her hair, Grima had relented. After all, she could see his point, people were curious as to why Kraka had no hair.

When Kraka's hair started to grow, it was more precious than Grima had remembered and she had almost insisted she cut it off once more. In the sunlight, it appeared Kraka's hair was spun from the sun itself. Her name, meaning raven, was certainly not fitting.

Even though she had allowed the long hair, Grima still insisted Kraka did not shower or wear fine clothes and so, even though they now had the wealth of the girl's father to cover such items, Kraka never benefitted from it. This morning she had been sent out into the fields in nothing more than rags.

"I understand how girls can be," Olaf replied. "I have three of them myself. Two are just approaching marrying age and I am nearly ready to send them off with the first men who come knocking at my door for them."

Grima laughed. "Yes, if Kraka were not so ugly, I would do the same thing. Unfortunately, I think my husband and I will be burdened with her for life."

"Ah, be thankful," Rolf responded. "I have one daughter and she is too embarrassed to even be seen with her father. I could never imagine the day where I was sick of the sight of her. Plus, if you married your daughter off, who would help out around here?" Rolf made a point of nodding towards Grima's hands. She disliked this man already.

"Yes, I suppose you are right," Grima replied even though

she wanted to ignore his comments. "Well, I am busy and need to return to the house. Please, sit out here and enjoy my hospitality while you wait for Kraka to return."

Grima turned and left then before she offended the king's men.

CHAPTER 11:

KRAKA

THE GOATS WERE ESPECIALLY FRISKY. KRAKA watched as they bounced and butted heads. It was fun to watch, for the first half of the morning at least, but eventually Kraka grew bored. She let the livestock tend to themselves for a moment while she trekked the short distance to the cliff edge.

The ocean was calm, unlike the goats she was tasked with watching. The sky and sea blended together at the horizon so it appeared impossible to tell where one ended and the other began. Kraka drew in deep breaths of the salty air. While she had grown up near the sea, Grima and Aki seldom let her down to the shore. She sighed. She could almost taste the tang of salt on her lips when she closed her eyes. How she wished she could go down there now and dip her feet in the cool waves as they gently nudged their way over the sand.

She opened her eyes and scanned the beach. The sight of a small fleet startled her. She shot a furtive glance back towards the goats, counting their heads without even being aware of it. They were all present. Their hound lounged comfortably under a lone tree, so it was obvious there was no immediate threat to the livestock. Kraka looked back to the ships.

It was not a huge fleet, but the longships were of an impressive size. Kraka counted them and noted that they all carried the same colours, indicating one person led them all.

Someone important, no doubt, she reasoned.

One man stood at the middle point of the ship and gazed ever out to sea. She suspected this was the leader of this group as no one seemed to approach him or bother him about tasks. The man intrigued Kraka. From what she could see, he was tall with hair the colour of wheat. She couldn't tell his age from the distance between them, but she studied him relentlessly as he gazed out to sea. A shout caused the man to turn and Kraka imagined he looked her way, seeing her, connecting with her. She ducked down. It was an instinct, to remain hidden from sight; Grima had always drummed that into her. Curiosity overcame fear, and she looked over the cliff once more.

He was gone, but Kraka saw a small speck of another man, shorter and darker, heading from the beach and up the path that lead to the farm at Spangareid. Could they be visiting with Grima and Aki? She felt her pulse quicken, hoping it was true.

She watched them for a while, noting that those on board seem settled and not yet ready to leave. So, perhaps they really were visiting with Grima and Aki. She couldn't work out why, but she knew an opportunity was being presented before her. She knew it in every fibre of her being.

Kraka stood taller, assessing the situation. She hated her life here with Grima and Aki, she knew they had murdered Heimir when she was very young, she remembered the event every night while she tried to sleep. She remembered her old name too, the one they had stolen from her along with her foster father. Yet, this name she still held onto, kept like a secret treasure in a box. When she couldn't sleep after those horrible dreams, she would coo her old name under her breath, using it like a talisman against her memories to soothe her into sleep once more.

While she behaved herself mostly around Grima and Aki, a resentment ran through her veins, making her want more. She wanted to leave this place, yet had been confined to it for so many years because she was fearful of being a young girl setting out on her own.

But now she was older, close to marrying age. Perhaps there was someone on those ships down there, bobbing gently at the shore, which would be happy to take her away to a new home filled with forests, farms, and adventure.

Her heart raced with the prospect of leaving Grima and Aki behind. Perhaps if she did, her nightmares would cease.

All at once, Kraka felt invigorated. She turned and charged away from the cliff end. The goats, sensing her excitement, gathered speed and flew around the field. Kraka strode forward in one determined direction, unlike the animals as they bumped and butted each other. She slowed as she reached the stream under a grove of trees.

Kraka decided to wash herself, even though Grima forbade her from doing so. She knew her foster mother well enough that if Kraka was to appear in front of the men clean and neat, Grima would not make a fuss in front of them.

She peeled off the rags she wore. Her skirt was dirty and her brown shift the wrong size. One elbow had been mended with green striped cloth. There was no mistaking the fact that Kraka was a peasant, even if she knew in her heart of hearts this wasn't true.

Kraka came from the Volsung clan, an old family line that was very prestigious, although they had descended into nothing more than herself at this present time. Even if she were the last standing Volsung, it was still a name that carried weight in her world.

Her heritage meant little, as she stood naked in the stream. What mattered more was how quickly she could clean herself and get back to the farm before her opportunity for a better life was snatched away from her.

She dove under the water and came up gasping for breath. The day was warm, yet the water was always icy here. Still, she persisted. She found some soapwort near the edge of the water. Using a rock, she pounded the roots of the plant before scouring her body and hair with it. She sluiced off in the cold water once more and repeated the process.

Once she felt she was clean enough, Kraka rose from the water and let the run dry her skin while she found a stick to help tease out the knots in her hair. While she did this, she picked over her clothes, working out how best to dress herself in order to be more appealing to a perspective suitor.

Her hair was dry and yet she still couldn't work out what she was going to do about her clothing. Kraka was worried she would miss the opportunity to be free of Spangareid. In the end, she just put it all back on, hoping her hair, which now hung down to the ground, would be a good enough distraction from her horrible outfit.

Kraka leaned over and looked at her dancing reflection in the water. Her cheekbones were high, distinct. Her eyes deep blue, like twilight. She had no idea if she was beautiful or not, since she could only compare herself to Grima, Aki and the people who lived close by. If she used them as a way to judge her appearance, she was spectacular. She doubted she was beautiful outside of the area though and wondered if there was a single man in the fleet on the beach that would be interested in her.

Quickly, she gathered up the goats and herded them back towards the farm. The animals were flighty, even with the dog present to keep them in line. It was as if they were channelling her nervous anticipation. When she reached the normal yard they were penned in, she found many of the goats would shy away from the opening. She used a long stick to help herd them together and, slowly, she managed to get them all through the gate.

Her hair tangled and twisted while she fought the excitable animals and, by the end of her battle, she had to stop and find another stick to help dig out the new knots. Once her hair was smooth again, she checked the gate again before heading towards the farmhouse.

"Kraka! Finally! We have guests." Grima's voice sounded agitated, although Kraka could tell she was trying to hide it from the others. Kraka smiled. So, the men from the ships were still here. She quickened her pace.

"Sorry, I am late. The goats just wouldn't be wrangled today." Kraka smiled as she spoke but her eyes darted around the group. Three men stood in front of her. They varied in age but all appeared fit and strong. This was in contradiction to their flour-dusted arms. "Who do we have here? Are they bakers?"

Looking towards Grima, her question was met with a steely gaze from her foster mother. Kraka had expected that, she knew just how much Grima tried to hide Kraka away and prevent her from looking her best. Having bathed and presented herself afresh had affronted the woman, Kraka knew. She smiled at her, not allowing Grima's bad mood decent on her. One of the men spoke in place of Grima.

"No, we are certainly not bakers. We are from Ragnar Lodbrok's fleet. Normally, we fight for our king. But, presently, we must bake for him since we have been away at sea for some time." The man was the oldest out of the group, his grey hair a mess of braids and his face bearing a smudge of flour.

"Well, Grima," said another of the men, this one younger, darker, closer to her in age. Perhaps he was the one she had seen heading up the path to their farm. Kraka instantly stepped a little closer to him. "You didn't tell us how beautiful your daughter was. Her name does not suit her at all. In fact, I can't believe a woman so beautiful is your daughter."

Grima huffed at the man. Her anger was hidden well from her face, Kraka noted, but she could tell it was there, thanks to the redness of her neck and the way she clenched her jaw before speaking. "This is what age and hard work does to beauty. Remember that well when your own wives start to complain their backs hurt and their hands ache from all their tasks. This is what they will become as old women."

The old man nodded. "It is so true, Grima. Beauty is as fleeting as youth is. It is hard for someone like Rolf to imagine now, but he will remember this conversation well when he is older, no doubt."

"Enough of the talk," Grima replied briskly. "Kraka, you need to help these men bake their bread. I have many tasks to attend to today, so cannot help. Plus, my hands are not up to the task of baking anyway."

And so Kraka was tasked with helping the men bake their bread.

CHAPTER 12:

RAGNAR

"YOU'VE BEEN GONE ALL DAY, HOW COULD you come back with only burnt bread?" Ragnar was angry. He paced back and forth between the contrite men, his face a blaze of red irritation.

"If I may speak, Ragnar?" It was Olaf.

"Please do, I can't wait to hear your story." Ragnar paused and glared at the man. He couldn't imagine what they would come up with to warrant the state of what they would have to eat for the next few days.

"It was because of a woman," Leif cut in. Ragnar turned to look at the young lad. A memory of seeing what he thought was the figure up on the cliffs earlier today darted across his mind.

"A woman? Out here?" Ragnar stretched out his arms as wide as they would go, to indicate the expanse of the land. I'm not even sure this is Norway!"

"Yes, even out here, there are women," Olaf expanded. "Although, their attractiveness varies considerably."

"That is the honest truth." Rolf snickered, slapping his leg for emphasis.

"Please, can someone explain to me what happened?" Ragnar could feel a headache coming on with the determined effort to keep his irritation under control.

Olaf stepped forward, his hands out in front, open, as if

he was trying to appease the king.

"Indeed, it was a woman, a very beautiful one, at that. I asked Leif to watch the loaves while they baked, but he was too distracted by this woman and let the loaves burn. When we cooked the second batch of loaves, the same thing happened. By then it was too late to start afresh. Perhaps we could stay another day to try again?"

Ragnar sagged a little. Olaf always offered a solution whenever a problem arose. It still didn't alleviate his frustration though. He was done with this place and just wanted to be on his way. Having spent the day watching the waves and waiting for the evening to approach, he was sick of the sight of the place. Sweden was not so far away and he was ready to meet with anyone other than the same crew he had seen for the entirety of this voyage.

"No woman is that beautiful, surely?" Ragnar questioned.

Leif stepped forward. "Oh, yes, I have never seen a woman as beautiful as this one. She had hair down to the ground and was as delicate as a bird. I freely admit that I could not help staring at her." Leif dropped his head, as if rueful of his actions.

"More beautiful than Thora?" Ragnar was intrigued now. He didn't believe a woman could be that stunning. His first wife had been considered the most attractive woman in all of Gautland. He had never come across another person who didn't admit her attractiveness was all-encompassing.

"No disrespect to your wife, Ragnar, but yes, I would say she is more beautiful," Rolf offered.

Ragnar was a taken back. Rolf would not be so stupid to say this woman was more stunning than his wife unless there was some merit to it. Ragnar stood and thought a moment.

"Alright then, if this woman is really as attractive as you

say, then you must bring her to me. If she is not as beautiful as you say, then I will punish the lot of you." Ragnar mad eye contact with each of the men then, making sure they understood he was serious.

"Oh, have no doubt, my king, this woman will not disappoint you," Olaf replied, as confident as the other two were. The three started to step back from Ragnar, as if he had dismissed them already.

"I am not finished yet," Ragnar interjected. "This woman must be brought to me neither clad nor unclad, neither fasting nor eating, and neither alone nor in company."

CHAPTER 13:

ᚲRAKA

OLAF AND ROLF RETURNED TO SPANGAREID just as the late afternoon began to blend into twilight. Kraka had seen them approach as she wiped out the dirty dishes while the evening meal cooked. She waited patiently until they scratched at the door. Stepping forward, she nearly made it there before Grima stepped out in front, blocking the way. Her foster mother threw open the door.

"You're back," she said. "Do you need to make more bread?"

"No," Olaf said. "King Ragnar has sent a message intended for your daughter, Kraka."

"Oh, really," Grima replied. Her words were slow, deliberate. Kraka knew the tone meant that she was irritated but still trying to contain her anger. She sidestepped Grima and placed herself between her foster mother and the two messengers from Ragnar.

"What is the message?" After the disastrous bread baking this afternoon, Kraka thought she would never see this fleet again. She was a little concerned about the message from the king though, and it instantly dampened her mood. Perhaps she was to be punished because of the bread. Although, she couldn't imagine why, it certainly wasn't her fault Leif had been so distracted.

Olaf relayed the message from the king. Once relief

flooded over her, she wanted to smirk. However, Kraka squashed it back, ready to play the most important game of her life.

"Please, tell your king that I couldn't possibly meet with him tonight, it is already beginning to darken. It would be improper for a girl like me to set foot on your ship this late in the day. People would talk. However, please tell King Ragnar that I will visit early on the morrow."

Olaf and Rolf left soon after that. They tried to persuade her to return with them and Kraka wondered if they were fearful to return without her. However, it didn't matter to her. Besides, she had to think things through first.

As soon as the door closed behind the men, Grima turned and stared her down. Kraka didn't break eye contact. Suddenly, she was no longer scared of this woman. Kraka would defend herself, escape, and race to the shore. She would join the fleet then—under any capacity. As soon as Olaf delivered Ragnar's message, Kraka knew that she wanted to be free of this place, that this night would be the last one she would spend here under the rule of Grima and Aki.

Grima was still staring at her. Kraka waited. Finally, when no footfalls or voices could be heard outside, the old woman spoke.

"Before you get any fanciful ideas in that head of yours, there is no way you can figure that riddle the king gave you. It is impossible and not meant to be broken. You are just a game to him, a distraction. They are probably all laughing and waiting to see what you try to come up with."

Kraka stared at Grima, her mouth agape. Her foster mother had always been blunt, but these words broke through her fantasy she had developed in her head and started to cut her down. For a moment it worked. Kraka pulled herself up and shielded herself from the woman's unkind words.

"You have no faith in me, Grima," Kraka replied. The words were quiet, small. Each word delivered was deliberate and forceful. "In the morning I will have the answer to this riddle and I will finally be free of this awful place. I will be free of you."

Kraka turned then, storming off to the corner of the farmhouse that she considered her own. She sank down into the furs there and closed her eyes.

She had to work the riddle out, she just had to, she thought.

Kraka didn't sleep as she tried to work out what to do, what Ragnar had meant when he said she needed to be "clad nor unclad, neither fasting nor eating, and neither alone nor in company."

Then, in the early hours of the new morning, the one in which she was supposed to meet with King Ragnar, Kraka broke the code. She smiled, excited by her discovery. Finally, she could sleep.

ᛦ

GRIMA WOKE KRAKA EARLIER than normal, as if she were eager to see her foster daughter's defeat. Instead, Kraka jumped out of bed, ready to grab her destiny in both hands and never let go.

"I need a net, Aki," Kraka said. "One of your trout nets. I also need a leek, Grima, and our dog."

"What on earth for?" Grima had asked. Aki said nothing but headed out the door. Looking out the window, Kraka watched as her foster father went to the small hut that housed all the trout nets. She turned back to Grima.

"The net will cover me, and so will my hair, yet I will also be unclad, just like King Ragnar requested. I will taste the leek, but not eat it fully, thus I will be neither hungry, nor full. If I take the hound with me, I will not be alone, yet no person will travel with me.

Grima gaped at her, surprise evident on her face.

"See, I am much smarter than you think, dear foster mother."

CHAPTER 14:

RAGNAR

RAGNAR ROSE EARLY THAT MORNING. TWO days of being idle had him filled with nervous energy at the prospect of seeing this woman of which his crew had boasted. He hoped she was stunning, like they said. He also wondered if she would be smart enough to work out his little riddle. While beauty was impressive, to Ragnar, intelligence was important as well. One night spent with a beauty would be fine too.

He stood on deck, trying to look busy as he unwound and rewound lengths of ropes. Those men who were already awake were trying their hand at fishing.

The sound of a dog barking drew Ragnar's attention to the path that led from Spangareid to the cove. He looked up, his hand instantly going to cover his eyes from the glare of sand.

He could see a figure approaching, long hair was whipping out in the wind, dancing around the woman's face so Ragnar would not see her properly as she approached. He rushed to shore as she approached.

"Hello." Ragnar called it out, eager to hear the woman speak. For he could tell, as she strode across the beach, that she was just as beautiful as Olaf, Rolf, and Leif had said to him the day before.

"Hello, King Ragnar." The woman stopped short and bowed her head slightly.

"I see you have worked out my riddle."

"Yes," she said as she took a bite out of a leek. "As you can see, I am neither clad nor unclad, hungry nor full, and, will my hound here; I am with company, yet also without it."

Ragnar was impressed. "Please, won't you step aboard my ship? I promise you that no harm will come your way."

He stepped forward to greet her, but the dog leapt at him, biting his hand. Without even being given time to reach for a weapon, Olaf stepped forward and stabbed the dog. It fell to the ground, instantly dead.

There was silence for a moment as everyone stared down at the animal. Finally, Ragnar lifted his gaze.

"I am sorry about your beast," Ragnar said as he wound his hand in a cloth Rolf gave him. "But, as I said, I cannot have any harm come to you."

The woman bowed her head once more. "Do not apologise, that dog is a herd dog, he has always been temperamental when it comes to humans. Although, it was likely protecting me and there was no reason to kill it."

"I am truly sorry then," Ragnar replied.

"No matter," Kraka replied. "Now, why don't you show me this impressive ship of yours?"

CHAPTER 15:

KRAKA

THEY TALKED THROUGH THE DAY AND Kraka couldn't believe how charming and handsome Ragnar was. As he spoke of his life growing up, and what it was like to be king, Kraka kept stealing furtive looks his way. His chiselled features astounded her.

However, it was more than Ragnar's obvious attractiveness. It was also the fact that she was sitting here, on a boat, entertaining a king. Two days earlier, she had been nothing more than a peasant girl that no one even knew about outside of her farm and the small village nearby. This is what really amazed her. She kept looking Ragnar's way to make sure he was real, that she wasn't just conjuring up the whole situation. In fact, twice she had pinched herself inconspicuously; in an attempt to convince herself she wasn't sleeping.

While Kraka knew her heritage and knew how important she was, no one else did. That Ragnar was seeking her out and didn't even know who she truly was surprised her. Maybe he just wanted someone to spend the night with, he was a man after all. To her, that seemed more likely than the preposterous notion he might actually be considering her as a suitable mate, since his first wife had been the daughter of an earl.

She gazed out across the broad expanse of ocean as she

wondered what other places and countries were like. Kraka couldn't imagine anything beyond Spangareid. Her notion of the rest of the world was confined to the fact she knew it was there and nothing more.

"Tell me about what it is like out there, across the ocean?"

"You have never been anywhere?" Ragnar asked. He turned; a quick quirk of his eyebrow was enough to show his amazement at this concept.

"I have been to the village square when we sell livestock," she replied. "Once, there was a trader from across the sea and he had linen patterned like I have never seen before."

There was silence. Kraka turned towards the king, her face open, honest. She looked up into his blue eyes and got lost in them. Her hand reached up, wanting to touch his face, his hair, but she stopped herself. Her own brazen words made her cheeks grow warm.

"I am amazed your parents have never taken you further afield, even within your own country. Norway is breathtaking." Ragnar's hand did reach up, more confident than her own was. He touched her hair, tucking a long strand back behind her ears. Kraka gasped with the contact. "Someone as beautiful as you should see the world."

Kraka ducked her head, embarrassed by his sweet talk. "I am not so sure about that. I have no one besides Grima to compare my looks to."

Ragnar's fingers reached under her shin. His delicate touch coursed through her as he tilted her head towards him. "Trust me, I have seen many women, and none compare to you besides my beloved Thora."

Kraka did not know what to say to that. The ghost of his deceased wife hung in the air between them, a reminder of all the king had lost.

But then, Ragnar was kissing Kraka and no words were needed anymore. His lips were warm, soft, and needy. Kraka had never kissed anyone before, but her body took over, igniting a passion within herself she never even knew existed. She gasped through the kiss, the shock of the contact and the way her body instantly reacted to Ragnar too much for her to bear. Ragnar broke away.

"I have startled you, I am sorry," he said, stepping back. His hand reached out and clasped the boat. Kraka did the same, needing the strong ship beneath her hands to support her in case her knees gave way. "Stay the night."

Ragnar said it softly as he gazed out over the ocean, a faraway look in his eyes. Then, he turned and Kraka could see the desire present there. She gasped again, hoping another kiss would come her way. She bit down on her bottom lip and her fingers dug into the palms of her hands as she tried to control herself. She wanted to throw herself at this man, to give herself up to him, completely, entirely, lose herself in his embrace.

Yet, she also knew she didn't want to be just a conquest of the king. Now that she had seen what was out there, beyond Spangareid, she didn't want to return to it. Oh, now she hated that place now. Grima and Aki too. It was as if Ragnar, through his kiss alone, had shown her the world and all the wonders in it. The last thing she wanted to do now was to turn her back on it all. Therefore, she needed to play a smart game, not a short one.

"I cannot, Ragnar," she replied. Each word was forced out through her teeth, her body vehemently against her mind's decision. "I will not be your conquest."

"I do not expect you to be. Come travelling with me instead, let me show you the world." Ragnar's eyes glittered as he turned to her.

Kraka was tempted. Oh, how she was tempted. Her body already craved this man, the one who had shared only a morning and a kiss with her.

"You need to see the world, and then decide if I am still the most interesting thing in it. Visit Sweden, and then come back here. If you return, I will be waiting for you."

Ragnar looked at her, really looked at her. Kraka thought it was as if he finally saw her for the very first time. She stared back at him, never wavering even though her insides were flipping, flopping, and trying to convince her head it was a fool. For the longest time they stood there, lost in each other's eyes.

Finally, he nodded. His decision made. "I will return Kraka, you will see. I have already seen so much of the world and know that you are the most beautiful thing left in it. Please, accept a gift from me, to prove this to you. Take one of Thora's shirts, one that I carry always with me to remind me of her scent. Take it as proof that I will return for you."

Kraka was stunned at his words. Maybe she really was more to him than a conquest. Surely he would not give out his dead wife's shirt to just anyone. She felt her words hitch in her throat, as if tears were going to replace them.

"I cannot take such a generous gift," Kraka said when the shirt was brought to her. It was a stunning piece of work, prettier than the fancy linen that trader had produced at the market. Kraka reached out and touched it, her fingers moving over the intricate details. The workmanship was exquisite. "This is much too beautiful for the likes of someone like me. You need to find someone of equal standing to wear it."

"I don't think that is possible," Ragnar replied. His eyes bore into her and the intensity frightened her for a moment, until she realised that her desire was equal to his.

"Please, keep the shirt, King Ragnar, and return after your trip to Sweden. If you don't, well, I shall go on. But I think you are settling on someone far beneath your standing if you do chance a return here."

Kraka turned, and looked out over the water again. The wind roared in across the ocean and buffeted her. She hoped Ragnar would think the salty air was the reason for her tears.

CHAPTER 16:

ℜAGNAR

"RAGNAR!" EYSTEIN WAS THERE TO GREET him when he finally arrived in Sweden. Ragnar jumped off the ship and gave Eystein a hug.

"Yes, here I am. How have you been?"

"Always the same, Ragnar," he replied. "It is always the same when you are a king, nothing but land disputes and marital disputes." Eystein winked and clapped Ragnar on the back.

"Ah, the life of a king, eh? I often wonder what it would be like to live merely as a peasant. There is much to be said to the simple lives of common folk."

Ragnar was thinking of Kraka when he said this. She had filled his mind endlessly during the journey. Ragnar had felt lonely as he drew away from Spangareid. His journey was a forlorn one as he contemplated his visit with King Eystein in Sweden. Instead, he had to visit with his old friend and exchanging niceties until enough time had passed so he could return to Kraka once more. So, here he was, making platitudes with the king of Sweden.

"Aye, I agree, Ragnar," Eystein replied. "I must admit, I have envied them on more than one occasion. Now, come inside, rest your sea-soaked feet and tell me about your wife."

Ragnar staggered. He had not expected Thora to be mentioned so early on in their conversation, nor had he considered the fact the news wouldn't travel before him. It felt like a physical blow. For the first time in days, his mind was pulled away from Kraka and the death of his first wife hit him fully.

"Thora is no longer in the land of the living." Ragnar managed to choke the words out.

"Oh, I am so sorry, Ragnar. Please, tell me what happened?"

"She got ill, it all happened very quickly. By the time I returned, she was already gone."

"Ragnar, welcome." A girl, around the same age as Ragnar's youngest son, Agnar, appeared in front of the main longhouse. She was leading a calf behind her. The animal was only half grown, but already Ragnar could see it was out of proportion. Its legs were longer than they should have been and it's head disproportionally sized to its body. The animal was likely to be huge as a result of this.

"Is this Ingibjorg?" Ragnar was welcome for the distraction away from Thora. "She grows so quickly. Before we know it, she will be bride-ready."

"Yes, I know. How our children are growing. And, before we know it, we will be old men and our grandchildren will be the ones earning all the glory."

Ragnar sighed. It seemed like only yesterday that the world was new to him and raiding was an eye-opener in regard to learning about the world around him. Yet, here he was, with children old enough already that he could sense his own mortality with more finality than ever before.

"My boys are already starting to learn about glory. I shudder to think how my old battle wounds will ache once they have had children. Already, it is an agony just to get up in the morning."

Eystein laughed at Ragnar and nodded his head in agreement.

"And, what of that beast? It will bring you a lot of meat someday," Ragnar said, ready to change the subject of old age.

"That is not a meat animal, Ragnar," Eystein replied. "We are raising it to become a great strategy in our battles one day. Eventually, it will win many wars for us."

"A cow?" Ragnar shook his head. "How much mead have you drunk already today?"

Ragnar slapped the king on the back of his neck and the pair laughed.

CHAPTER 17:

RAGNAR

RAGNAR TRAVELLED QUICKLY AFTER KRAKA left. His need to visit with Eystein in Sweden was now nowhere near as important as returning quickly to Kraka's side. After all, what if someone else discovered her at Spangareid and took her as his own before Ragnar returned there? He couldn't bear the thought of another man snatching this woman out from under his nose.

Therefore, his journey had been as brief as it needed to be without seeming abrupt. Eystein and Ragnar had spent many days together, talking and rekindling their ties. They had been friends since childhood, so Ragnar was glad Kraka had insisted he continue on to Sweden as he had first intended. However, he was also glad once the visit was over and he was back on his ships heading for Norway once more.

It was approaching dark when his fleet reached the shores of Spangareid, so he immediately sent a messenger to speak with Kraka. He waited nervously, as if he were a mere young boy again anticipating word from his first potential girlfriend.

"Ragnar!" Olaf called his name as soon as he returned to the beach. Ragnar jumped down off the boat and rushed forward.

"How does Kraka fair?" He was worried another suitor had snatched her away from him while he was absent. It had been the single constant worry of his since he left this shore, a month earlier. When he should have been worrying about threatening storms, all he thought of was Kraka lying with another man. As he convened with Eystein, as they renewed their alliance, all that came to his mind was the way Kraka had looked out over the water before she told him to find someone else. Perhaps she wasn't really interested in him? Maybe she had been trying to put him down gently. Ragnar didn't know what to think, only that he had to try this one last time to engage with the beautiful and mysterious woman that seemed so out of place in Spangareid.

During his time away, his crew, while understanding of how Ragnar could be attracted to someone as stunning as Kraka, were dubious as to why he would be so eager to marry below his standing. Those brave enough, usually after a skin of wine, had brought it up with the king. Ragnar was unsure of his conviction at those times. Wondering if he was simply a fool for wanting to marry one based on beauty and wit rather than standing, suspecting he was.

"Kraka is well, King Ragnar," Olaf answered. "She will meet with you on the morrow; however, as she fears it is too late to meet in person tonight."

A fleeting moment of despair mixed with irritation washed over Ragnar. A small part of him was mad that she kept pushing him aside all the time. He was a king, after all and her nothing more than a lowly peasant. Kraka should be running to him, giving him everything he pleased because she would likely never get another offer like this. The snake of doubt slithered in after that. Perhaps she was brushing him off after all. Maybe she wasn't interested in him. That thought made him cringe. Was he just a fool chasing someone like Kraka, who seemed so self-assured even though she came from nothing? Was he even really doing her a favour? Would she really be better off in his world rather than out here on the fringes of it where life was much more honest? All of these questions whirled around in his mind as his stomach knotted up with doubt.

"But what of her answer?" Ragnar finally asked, ready for the brunt of her rejection. "Did she say she would come away with me?"

"Aye, she did," Olaf answered instantly. Ragnar's heart leapt up into his throat. His doubt dissipating as he felt his knees weaken in relief, even as he sagged slightly; he wanted to run the length of the beach. Nervous energy was consuming him and he wasn't sure how to deal with it all. Ragnar controlled himself as years of kingly duty instinctively took hold. He smiled briefly at Olaf and turned back to the ship, pretending that his world had not just changed so dramatically.

CHAPTER 18:

𝕶RAKA

WHEN OLAF ARRIVED, KRAKA MET HIM AS SHE brought in the goats. She had been far away from the farmhouse and her foster parents, so they had no idea their world was about to change.

As she settled in for the night, she still kept her little secret. She wanted to hold onto it as long as possible, only to reveal it at the moment of her departure. While she wanted to see the looks of shock on their faces right at the moment she left, she also had practical reasons. Kraka knew that as soon as she revealed her intentions, Grima and Aki would try to stop her from going. They needed her here to help run the farm now they were so old. If she told them too early, she was worried what they would do to keep her there. She remembered what they did, all those years ago, to Heimir and knew they were capable of anything for the sake of their own comfort and happiness.

While grey dread settled over her like a rain cloud, Kraka tried to distract herself from worrying about what Grima and Aki would do in the morning. She attempted to imagine what it would be like to be a queen alongside Ragnar Lodbrok and couldn't even begin to fathom what it would entail. Would she have slaves to tend to her? How did she even feel about that? After all, she was nothing more than a slave herself. Ragnar didn't realise that, though. He still thought Grima and

Aki were her real parents. Kraka was too scared to reveal who they were for fear Ragnar would reject her. A peasant was infinitely better than a slave was, after all.

She hadn't revealed her true identity to Ragnar either. Kraka couldn't work out why she was so hesitant to tell him the truth. Maybe it was the ever-pervading fear she carried on from Heimir that her line was destined to be eradicated. Or, maybe, she wanted to be loved for herself and not her lineage. Kraka didn't know. Once more, doubt clouded in so she busied herself with discreetly packing her meagre belongings.

She stole through the house while Aki was away packing barley into the barn, the same barn Heimir had been slaughtered in. Without even being aware, a quick sob erupted from Kraka's throat when she thought of that. She swallowed it back though; too busy in her need to pack her satchel before Grima returned from the root cellar with stores for the night's evening meal. She felt the cold dread of possible discovery every time a board squeaked under her feet. Did Grima hear her moving stealthily around the house, she wondered as she pulled out a cloak and stuffed it into her bag?

A creak on the cellar steps told Kraka that Grima was returning. The bulky cape fought with her bag, as if it were on Grima's side and wanted Kraka to be caught. Hot tears of frustration welled up as she battled with the material. Realising it was the cloak pin that was the enemy; she yanked it free and continued to wrestle with the item. Each creak of the steps below caused her more frustration but, finally, the cloak was in the satchel and Kraka had barely enough time to push the bag under her furs before Grima walked through the door. She hid the cloak pin in the sleeve of her robe and hoped Grima would not notice her awkward stance.

The cape pin was she had always owned. Even Grima and Aki didn't dare take it from her. She never wore the pin, as it was too beautiful for everyday use. It bore an image of a sword and a dragon, a reminder of who her real father was. Kraka ran her fingers over the fine silver. It was the most beautiful thing she owned, in fact, the most beautiful thing she had ever seen.

After they had prepared and eaten the evening meal, Kraka retired to her end of the house. She deposited some food she had coveted while Grima was busy. She didn't need it, but she took it anyway, more out of spite for Grima and Aki than any real need for it. After all, Ragnar would now be providing for her.

All of her clothes went into the bag as well. She only had two outfits and one pair of shoes, but she would not leave them behind for Grima to make use of them. For all the years she had lived with them, Kraka still had an underlying hatred brewing for the pair. They had killed the one person left in this world that cared about her. While they had allowed her a life, they had never been kind to her. She felt no need to be thankful for her existence under them.

She hadn't asked for them to take Heimir from her, even if her life had been confined while she was with him. Heimir had loved her like his own daughter, Grima and Aki hadn't, seeing her only as someone who could do the work they were no longer able to.

As her freedom bore down on her, her hatred grew like the fire Grima now tended as Kraka placed the last item into her bag. It was a ring, her mother's ring, Heimir had said. Kraka had always hidden this one item away from Grima and Aki. While they seemed to look on the Dragon pin with some sort of superstition, a gold ring was always a gold ring, something to be traded for whatever they liked. Kraka pulled it free from its hiding place between the lose boards of the farmhouse. She wanted to wear it but was too afraid Grima would see it before she had left with Ragnar. Instead, she tucked it into her satchel and tried to be patient. Kraka could wear it tomorrow. She would never have to take it off after that.

$$\Psi$$

THE MORNING CAME AT such a slow pace that Kraka thought she was dreaming its arrival at first. She had lain in bed until the middle of the night trying to sleep, tossing and turning until Grima had scolded her. After that, Kraka had held her body rigid, willing herself to sleep. Each time her body started to twitch, she held herself tight, willing herself still again. Eventually her wish for sleep must have been granted. However, she must have only slept a few hours because when she opened her eyes, feeling excited and refreshed, it was still dark.

Kraka lay there, as steady as she could, waiting for light to creep into the house. When it did, she pinched herself, wondering if she had fallen back asleep and was now dreaming again. Still she waited, as the light crept in and helped waken her foster parents.

When Grima rose from her bed, Kraka jumped up, ready to announce her news.

"Grima, Aki, you need to listen to this, I have such exciting news!" The words rushed out as Grima frowned at her and Aki sat up, looking confused.

"What are you talking about, Kraka?" Grima growled at

her. "You need to bring in some wood to get this fire started."

"Get it yourself, Grima, I am done with this place." Kraka smiled broadly at Grima as she spoke the words. "Ragnar has returned and I am to leave with him today, bound across the sea to become his queen."

There was silence as the words sunk in. They knew she wasn't lying, they had discussed her meeting with Ragnar all those weeks ago in great detail, asking her over and over again what they had said to each other and how serious she thought his intentions were. They weren't doing it because they were interested in her happiness or the prospect of her gaining such a respectable suitor. Instead, they had fretted over her leaving. Because of this, Kraka had left out much of what Ragnar and she had really spoken about and gave no hint that Ragnar might return for her. They were happy when she suggested he was merely sniffing around her for fun. Now, Kraka was excited to announce what Ragnar had really wanted from her. She also shared her own intentions.

"But, have no fear, dear foster parents; I have some parting words for you." Kraka took advantage of their stunned silence to edge her way towards the door. She needed to say her piece and be clear of the house so she could escape. She could run faster than either Grima or Aki, but she needed to be free of the house and the closed door behind her before she could flee properly. "I know what you did to Heimir, all those years ago, even though you think I had forgotten. Just because I never spoke of my foster father, the one who really did care about me, it doesn't mean I didn't remember."

"Kraka." Aki said. It was one small word, like a frightened baby bird squawking for its parent. Kraka had stared at Aki, when she mentioned Heimir being the foster father that loved her and she saw the wound it made. Even though Aki had killed Heimir, Kraka knew that he felt guilt over it more than Grima ever did. Grima mostly laughed when she thought her and Aki were in private and discussing Heimir.

"Yes, I suppose that is still my name now," she replied, leaning forward. "Or perhaps I will tell Ragnar the truth about who you really are and what you did all those years ago.

Grima went pale then. Kraka had hit a nerve it seemed. "Please, Kraka, you know I loved you like a daughter."

Kraka laughed at the lie.

"Don't worry, Grima, I will not tell Ragnar the truth. Not yet, at least. Instead, I will make a vow to you. I know you killed Heimir, but you did not kill me, even though you had the chance. For that, I will not repay the favour. However, please know that, as I stand here, each day that you both continue to live will be worse than the day before it. And, this is why I will not tell Ragnar about what you did. Instead, I will let you live a long life each so that as each day becomes worse and worse, you will beg for death, and beg for mercy. Instead, you will just be given more suffering." Kraka stood tall then, feeling the echo of the Volsung line as it flowed through her, drawing on the blood of her valkyrie mother and channelling the wisdom of knowing that she knew she possessed. "Your last day, however, will be unlike any of the prior days of your time on earth. Your last day alive will be the very worst you have ever felt."

With that final prophecy, Kraka opened the door to the farmhouse and strode through, ready to meet her new destiny. The ones the gods were giving her now on account of all the suffering she had endured up to this point.

CHAPTER 19:

ＫRAKA

KRAKA STRODE FROM HER CLOISTERED existence, the day blooming warm with the clouds clearing as she marched towards the beach. She felt alive, as if she had been dead before today and was only now being born into the life she was supposed to live.

When she reached the beach, Ragnar was there to greet her, reaching out to clasp her hand as she boarded the ship. He drew her in, enclosing her in his strong arms. Kraka allowed herself to be absorbed by him, letting their bodies mingle. She cried then, quiet tears that soaked through Ragnar's shirt. He pulled her back, confused at the sight of them.

"What's wrong?" he asked.

"Nothing," Kraka replied. "Absolutely nothing. These are happy tears." Kraka spoke the honest truth.

He put his arm around her shoulder, drawing her back into his warmth, making her feel like she had finally found a home here, by his side. He guided her over to the bow and they watched as the ship readied to leave.

"Your parents are not here to see you off?" Ragnar asked.

Kraka just shook her head, not able to answer through all her happy crying. Ragnar didn't question her further and she hoped he assumed the lack of her parents was another reason for her tears.

They stood there, for a long time, watching the crew get the ship ready to travel. Then, while they launched the boat, Kraka eventually turned, watching the land slip away. As Spangareid shrunk from her sight, her tears diminished, whipped away by the breeze as it kicked up and the remains dried with the glaring sunshine. It couldn't be more perfect weather to sail away from her childhood hell and Kraka smiled until it felt like her face would crack.

Once the land disappeared from sight, Kraka turned again, and watched the new horizon, her new horizon. She didn't know where they were going. In fact, she didn't even care. Anywhere was better than where she had come from.

Olaf approached. "Your quarters are readied, King Ragnar." The man left after Ragnar nodded at him.

"What about mine?" Kraka asked.

Ragnar turned to her. He looked surprised. "You will sleep with me, will you not?"

Kraka looked at him, then out to sea. Oh, how she wanted to join him in his quarters that night. She had dreamed of sex every night since Ragnar had left for Sweden. Yet, now here she was, shy at the thought of it.

But, there was more to it than that. Kraka was scared. Not from the physicality of sex, she had seen the fundamentals of it with Grima and Aki in such small quarters. No, sex didn't scare her, it was the ricocheting implications of the act that made her pale. She knew that babies and birthing was dangerous, but that wasn't the worst of it. Giving herself up entirely to another person, loving him and being vulnerable to him, was what terrified her. What if she loved him implicitly and then he died, like Heimir had? She couldn't stand that sort of betrayal again. Yet, it wasn't any of those things that truly settled her decision. In fact, part of it she couldn't even explain to Ragnar just yet, not without sounding completely mad.

"I will not lay with you, Ragnar, not until we are married. I hope you understand that." Kraka turned, making eye contact with him. She stared at him honestly, openly, and felt more vulnerable in that moment than if she had been standing there naked in front of all the crew.

She hoped Ragnar would not be so offended with her suggestion that he set her down in the first port they came to. She wanted this to work, above all else. Yet, she needed to know that Ragnar loved her more than just as a flight of fancy while he travelled. Her whole life had seen her as a burden, Kraka felt. First, when her parents died and Heimir took over as her foster father. He had been happy to look after her, she knew this, yet, she had been a worry to him. Heimir had given up his standing in order to protect her. Then, Grima and Aki took over when they killed Heimir. They hadn't really wanted her, and helped Kraka to understand this not only by telling her, but by making sure she was laden with all of the tasks on the farm they didn't want to do.

Over the years, the sense of burden had grown within Kraka, seething and developing into something so huge that she was sure Ragnar would also think she was a weight on him eventually. She was scarred, damaged by her very existence. Part of her was trying to push Ragnar away by setting unreal expectations in an effort to shelter her from him and his realisation that she was now his problem to bear. Another part of her hoped that Ragnar would rise above that, see her hurdles as challenges he would accept gladly. Kraka hardly dared to believe that Ragnar might see it this way and meet her obstacles head on, relishing the challenge of proving to her how much she meant to him.

As Kraka stared at Ragnar, she could see his conflict. He wanted to lay with her, that was evident. She knew the crew would know if they didn't sleep together and she wondered if they would tease him as a result. Kraka felt like folding. She wanted to tell him it was all right, that she was only teasing him. But then, Ragnar opened his mouth to speak.

"Oh course, Kraka," he said. "It was awfully presumptuous of me to assume you would join me as though we were married. There is plenty of time for that once we return home and I wed you properly."

Kraka was surprised, her lips parted, spreading wide in a grin she could not control. She leapt at Ragnar, throwing herself into his arms and hugging him with wild abandonment.

"Thank you for understanding, Ragnar. Your heirs will thank you." She pulled away, and then dove in for a kiss. Ragnar kissed her back as he laughed at her.

"You're getting ahead of yourself there with heirs, aren't you?"

"Not at all," she replied. "Imagine if I fell pregnant on board this ship? Our child would not have proper heritage rights like subsequent children would, you know that. It would be unfair on that first child, for the sake of a week's voyage."

"Woman, how many children are you expecting to have?" Ragnar laughed again. It was a bellow of a noise this time, unrestrained and joyous.

Kraka looked at him earnestly. "I have the gift of sight. I know things like this."

Ragnar's laugh stopped dead. He was still smiling as he looked at her, but his interest was piqued.

"Many people say they have the sight." He looked at her more closely, his eyebrows knitting together as if he was seeing something that intrigued him. "But, I think you are telling the truth here. Does Grima have the sight? Is that who you get it from?"

It was Kraka's turn to laugh. "No, I do not get it from Grima, but another female relative." She wanted to tell him who Grima really was, but she remembered the prophecy she left her foster parents with and felt the need for them to suffer for as long as she had. If she told Ragnar now—all of her story—then he would turn the ship around to deal with them, of that she had no doubt. Kraka didn't want her foster parents lives shortened before they had a chance to really feel the misery of her absence. So, she remained silent. Instead, she drew the conversation away from her lineage. "I see many children in our marriage."

Ragnar smiled when she said that. For what king wouldn't be happy with those words?

CHAPTER 20:

ᚴRAKA

THEIR JOURNEY WAS UNEVENTFUL AFTER that first day. Kraka was thankful for this as she enjoyed the burden that was beginning to lift from her shoulders. It was one she never even knew existed. She was thankful Ragnar considered her in all aspects, whereas her foster parents never had. When she broached the fact she did not want to sleep with him until they were married, even though her body had rebelled against the idea—and she knew his did too—she was thankful Ragnar was in agreeance on the matter. It was a surprise, after all these years, that she could have a conversation without an argument when her idea differed from the other person. It was even more surprising that her thoughts were even considered to start with. It was something she could get used to, though, she decided.

Their wedding commenced as soon as they arrived in Ragnar's kingdom. He announced it loud and clear, let no one question Kraka's heritage, and she was ever thankful for this. Kraka knew there were people who would be furious at Ragnar's choice of a peasant for a bride. However, considering his first marriage had already produced sons, she supposed there was less of a need to produce heirs. Still, even if people didn't like his choice, Kraka was used to having people resent her position. It had gotten her parents killed after all.

Kraka met Ragnar's sons not long after they alighted. Eirek and Agnar were fine boys, nearly as old as she was, and just as handsome as their father.

She embraced them. "I am so happy to finally meet the sons of my new love. I hope you both grow to love me as your stepmother. However, I do not want you to love me as you did your mother, because I don't want to replace her in your eyes."

One of the boys softened at her words, the older of the two, Eirek. Agnar, on the other hand, seemed to close himself off even more at the mention of his mother by his father's soon to be new wife. He pulled back from the embrace and turned away. Kraka totally understood and left him alone.

The wedding feast commenced that evening and tied in with Ragnar's welcoming feast. Kraka was introduced to many people; more than she ever thought had existed in the world, let alone in one place. She felt weary with trying to remember all of their names. When she was offered more wine, she took it gratefully. Although, she didn't want to drink too much, for she knew, with the whispers of a new premonition about her and Ragnar's first-born child, that she needed to keep a level head about herself tonight.

"Well, wife," Ragnar said, in the midst of the merriment. No one took any notice of them anymore since so much wine had been poured. Kraka felt the intimacy of the moment even though they were in the middle of a loud and crowed room. "How does it feel to be a queen?"

Ragnar nuzzled her neck as he spoke and Kraka melted into his touch. She wanted to touch him, run her hands all over his body, and kiss him repeatedly until it was morning. Kraka put her glass of wine down. She needed to stop drinking, she realised. Her body was taking control of her head.

"I have no idea yet, dear husband," she replied. Smiling at him and allowing herself to partake of a kiss. "Ask me again the next time the moon is full and I have had the chance to step into a queen's shoes for a while."

"A wise answer," he replied. However, he seemed more distracted by pushing aside her hair and kissing her shoulder than her answer. "I cannot wait to lay with you tonight."

Kraka froze. Ragnar noticed and stopped what he was doing. He sat up straight and looked at her.

"The prophecy," she explained when he raised an eyebrow at her in question. "The one I had about us having so many children had a second part to it. I fear that we must not lie together for a further three days, or our first child will bear an illness."

"Are you playing with me, woman?" Ragnar laughed his reply, but Kraka knew there was a serious question behind the mirth. "It seems we will never get to know each other except for talking."

Her face sagged. Kraka knew he was discontent, she could see it in the indecision flickering on his face, the slight twitch at his eye and the way he held his mouth tight. She understood the frustration for she felt it too. However, who was she to go against the gods? Kraka knew in her core, the very part of her that had come from Brynhildr—the valkyrie blood—that what she said was true. There would be a great calamity if she and Ragnar were to lie together as true husband and wife tonight on their wedding night.

"The gods will it, Ragnar," she finally said. "I cannot go against the gods, you must understand that. It is only for a few more nights, and what is that, really, after the time we have already spent together?"

Ragnar looked at her, his blue eyes bearing into her, making her resolve slip even as she felt the power of the gods welling up inside of her. Somehow, Ragnar's pull seemed greater than the gods did. When she had been speaking earlier to one of the earls under Ragnar, he had mentioned the story about how Ragnar was descended from Odin, the Allfather. Kraka could understand that now, as she gazed at him, losing herself within the deep pools of his eyes. She wanted to throw caution to the wind just from this single gaze, his mere touch. She had barely been with him for any great length of time. Imagine the power he wielded when he really had time to work his magic, she thought. No wonder he had such influence across the lands, and from such an early age.

Kraka shivered. The gods were present, here in the room with them all right now; she could feel their manifestation even if she couldn't see them. She wrapped her arms tight around herself, bracing against their will. Kraka just wanted to lose herself to her new husband, the one who had been so patient already. She couldn't understand this need, this desire, to go against what she knew was fated. Or, perhaps, that was it. Perhaps what happened tonight, what she suspected was going to happen was already fated, the gods already decreeing it and leaving the internal battle for her alone. Kraka didn't like the way her thoughts were going. How dare she justify away a child's impending illness because she couldn't wait three more days to lay with her husband. And yet, every time she glanced over at Ragnar, got lost in his mesmerising gaze, she felt like what she wanted to do was the right thing. She looked at him, his eyes her entire world.

Her resolve strengthened as a man approached and spoke to Ragnar. Once the spell of his alluring eyes was broken,

Kraka sat taller and felt the will of the gods strengthening within her. She was determined to make Ragnar wait. She had to. After all, she did not wish ill of her firstborn child.

Then Ragnar turned back to her, his hands wandering, claiming her as she sat there, staring out across a room of strangers. His fingers delved and searched as they had on so many nights already. He had opened her to passion, even if they had not made love yet. Kraka had no idea she was capable of such wanting and yearning until Ragnar was let loose on her body. She groaned into his touch, her eyes closing as she felt herself wavering again.

Ragnar had been so patient, she reasoned. He had travelled the whole voyage across the sea without pushing her further than she was willing to go, once she had set the boundaries on her first day aboard his ship. He had never pressured her, never pushed her and Kraka was thankful. She had left her life behind on a whim and a promise and here she was, making King Ragnar wait for what likely seemed indefinitely to him. If she were Ragnar, she would be mad already. Or, even wondering if she were being strung along for some other purpose.

Kraka, without even thinking, took a deep drink from Ragnar's cup while his hands worked their magic on her body. She regretted it as soon as she swallowed, knowing how strong the wedding-mead was. Yet, she knew she had no control over the matter. It was as if her hand had taken over, willed by the gods and beyond her logical reasoning.

She shuddered and Ragnar mistook it for ecstasy. He smiled at up at her and nestled his lips into her neck once more.

"I cannot wait to taste you, down there." He whispered the words yet they were powerful enough to smother her resolve. She felt it dissolving away from her, every last doubt of what they should or should not be doing tonight and let her body—and instinct—take over.

Ragnar sensed it; she knew he did. For, after that, he stood, lifting her up and throwing her over his strong shoulder like she were nothing more than a fur to keep him warm.

The crowd cheered and threw out lewd comments as Ragnar strode from the room with his new wife.

$$\Psi$$

THE FURS WERE LUXURIOUS as Ragnar laid her down upon them, welcoming her as she sunk into them. Kraka felt her head swim. It was not only from the alcohol, but from the heady feeling of finally letting herself go, giving herself up to another person and not caring one little bit about the consequences of her actions.

Ragnar's hands roamed, touching all the spots he had already learned would awaken her. Kraka moaned and her eyes closed as she let herself go with the sensations. Finally, his hands reached up, and unlaced her robe. She let him do it. He had never seen her fully naked before now and Kraka felt a slight pause, like she should stop this somehow. Then, her breasts were exposed and Ragnar was there, licking her nipples and blowing on them and she couldn't rationalise another thought beyond the yearning that coursed throughout her body.

Ragnar pulled her robe completely off and stood, staring down at her nakedness. Opening her eyes, Kraka stared back at him, her husband. She couldn't believe her luck, after all these years of hell, here she was, about to start a wonderful new life with a king.

Then Ragnar took his own clothes off and kissed her in places she never thought lips would travel to and she lost herself all over again.

CHAPTER 21:

ᚱRAKA

"AGNAR!" KRAKA CALLED HER STEPSON'S name out across the marketplace. She had been trying to crack his cool exterior since she arrived a month ago. He had been distant and somewhat surly towards her on many occasions and she was done with it.

"I am busy," Agnar replied.

She wouldn't take no for an answer. "Your father has instructed you show me around town." They had been discussing Agnar's aversion to Kraka this morning and Ragnar had decided she should just take the boy aside and have a quiet word with him. There was no need for Agnar to be unkind to his stepmother, and Kraka took it personally when he ignored her or muttered under his breath when she spoke to him.

"Haven't you learnt your way around yet?"

"No."

Agnar huffed and rolled his eyes at her but Kraka didn't care. At least he had agreed to accompany her without too much dispute.

"Where is it you wish to find?" he finally asked.

"The hut where they dye the linens." Kraka had a basket of plain linen and she really did want a crimson cloak, deep and red as blood. However, she already knew that the building was across the marketplace in a quiet corner where the strong smells would be less obvious.

"Very well then." Agnar led the way and Kraka had to hurry to keep up with him. As soon as they were clear from the noise and bustle, Kraka reached out and grabbed his arm.

"I would like a quiet word please." She looked at the boy, already old enough to fight and to marry. He was tall and blonde like his father, but his eyes were dark, apparently like his grandfather, Herrud. "I know we have gotten off to a bad start, Agnar. I am not sure why, but I want to tell you something about myself, if you will allow it?"

Agnar stared at Kraka, a blush tainting his face. Kraka saw the opening she needed.

"If you must, Queen Kraka."

She was taken back by her regal title. It still didn't sit easily on her shoulders, even after a month of being called it. Even after Ragnar had fought against those who said she was only a peasant and not worthy of the title. Kraka ignored her discomfort and took the opening offered to her.

"I was raised on a farm. Yes, I am a peasant." She wished she could tell Agnar about her horrible foster parents and how she understood what it was like to have someone step in on behalf of someone you loved and how they could never replace that person. But, she couldn't. Ragnar still didn't know the truth about Grima and Aki. "I do not know the ways of royal life, that is true. However, I am not here to step into your life and replace your mother. I don't want to do that, and I certainly can tell you do not want me to do it either. So, we need to find some sort of compromise, because I do not wish to be your enemy."

Agnar stood still. Kraka watched and waited, wondering if he was going to storm off. Eventually, though, he spoke to her.

"I do not think of you as my enemy." His voice was quiet and he refused to look at her. "I just feel like it's too soon for my father to be with another woman." He blushed, obviously embarrassed at the admission.

"I'm sorry for that, Agnar. But, the heart cannot be told how soon it is before you can love again. I know your father still misses your mother terribly. I have woken in the night to the furs wet with his tears and Ragnar saying her name in his sleep. He suffers terribly that he was not present when she died and I wish it had been different, so that he could have been here for you when Thora died."

There was silence then. Kraka barely dared to breathe as she waited for Agnar to respond. His face was contorting slightly, like he might shout at her, but then, he turned and ran. Kraka thought she head a sob tear from him as he left.

Ψ

THE WALK TO THE dyeing hut was pleasant enough and Kraka was preoccupied as she made her way there, Agnar on her mind as she walked.

"Hello!" A male voice called out, distracting Kraka. She looked up, wondering if it was meant for her. A hand clapped down on her shoulder. She turned; ready to admonish whoever had dared to touch her. She may be new to her title, but she was already aware that not just anyone could reach out and touch her.

"Eirik!" Kraka smiled when she realised who it was. Ragnar's other son to Thora was the polar opposite of Agnar in regard to how he treated her.

"Where are you going?"

"To colour some linen," Kraka explained. "Would you like to walk with me?"

"Of course." Eirik settled in comfortably beside her, his height and stance reminding her of Ragnar as they walked. She almost reached out to clasp his hand before remembering this was not her husband. She glanced at him, to remind herself that Eirik was so young, and much darker in colouring than his father was.

"What have you been up to today?" She found their conversation flowed more easily than it ever did between her and Agnar. As a result, Eirik regaled her with all of his adventures for the day. They amounted to nothing more than weapons training and teasing the local girls, but with the way Eirik explained it, it seemed so much more exciting.

They reached the hut before she was ready to see her stepson leave. He made her day interesting in a new world filled with strangers. Besides her husband, Eirik was the only other person that made her feel like she belonged here, as if she had always been a part of this bustling society.

She sighed as Ragnar's son bounded off towards a group of young maidens and left her there, moving into the street and out of her sight as she turned to enter the building.

CHAPTER 22:

ＫRAKA

WHEN IT WAS ANNOUNCED KRAKA WAS pregnant, Ragnar's kingdom rejoiced, even those that had called her a peasant behind her back. Eirik had leapt forward to hug her, others cheered in celebration. Some there may not have agreed with Ragnar's choice in a bride, however, babies were always welcomed, especially those belonging to the king.

Kraka, on the other hand, did not. Of course, she was excited to be pregnant so soon, bearing what she knew would be a son for the king. However, she remembered the prophecy every moment of each day. She knew what the consequences of her and Ragnar not waiting would be, and she was saddened by their actions and what this would bring to their unborn child.

Ever since she had awoken, the day after their wedding feast, Kraka had regretted her night of passion. She still couldn't believe she had fallen so easily for Ragnar's charms. The night had been worth it, she still felt slivers of desire when she thought about their lovemaking. However, she also felt she had failed her firstborn child.

Ragnar had been exuberant when he awoke that morning. He smiled at her and gathered her up in his arms when she wept about their mistake.

"You cannot fight the gods, Kraka, you know that, and I know that. This night was fated already and you could not have denied the gods wishes as pull the stars out of the sky just by looking at them."

Kraka felt better when Ragnar pointed this out, knowing he was telling the truth. Their lives were decided by the gods before they were even born. She rubbed her belly and realised this child's problems were also already fated by the gods. It was a mystery why the gods let her know what could have been had she resisted her husband's advances on their wedding night. Her child could have been healthy, had they just waited a few more nights before consummating their union.

They had made love then. Ragnar kissed her, loved her, and made her forget for a while that they had made a grievous error so early on in their marriage.

After that night, Kraka had approached Ragnar often, ready to be consumed by passion so she could forget their mistake. So, that Ragnar could remind her that their fates were already decided and her knowing couldn't have changed it regardless.

Over the coming months, while their passion ignited, Kraka slowly started to pull away from her guilt. Ragnar's love embraced her, warmed her, made her feel more loved and cared for than she had ever thought possible. And so, the fates had taken over, replacing her doubt with the knowledge that their child was important, that he was to be special, even if he was born with a disability.

She knew, even as a disabled child, their son would be a great man one day. The gods had finally allowed that knowledge to filter through to her. It drowned out her doubt and misgivings at their wedding night and finally, at the birth of her first child, she welcomed his arrival and all of his complications as a result.

"His name is Ivar," Ragnar announced the day after his son's birth.

Ψ

HE WAS EXUBERANT IN front of everyone, but Kraka knew he was crestfallen about his son. As it had been predicted, Ivar was born with gristle where his legs should have been. He howled, as if in pain, through the night, his lungs as strong as a beast in the field. However, his strength didn't stop there. Even though his legs weren't properly formed, it was as if the rest of his body had absorbed what power should have been stored there and evenly distributed it. Kraka smiled at his strength, knowing the rest of him would make up for his lack of bones in his legs.

Now it was time for Kraka to comfort her husband and remind him that the gods had decreed this and they had really no choice in the matter, all those moons ago on their wedding night.

Sometimes he turned on her, accusing Kraka of magic that made Ivar like this as punishment for Ragnar sleeping with her when she said they couldn't. Kraka had been shocked. She felt all the colour bleed from her face and her legs shook like she were about to collapse. Instead, a rage had burned up through her being and Kraka had flown at him, wanting to hit and hurt him the way he had just done to her.

Over time, Kraka became used to his bluster. Ragnar may have wondered if she was a witch, but his insecurities stemmed not from her, but from himself. After that first time, when Kraka was so visibly upset by his words, he usually backed away, sitting down and sobbing, begging to the gods and asking why they had not prevented him from sleeping with Kraka on their wedding night.

Her heart softened then and she rushed to him, hugging him tight and telling him all those things he had once told her, while she was still pregnant with Ivar. Eventually her words would appease him and the angry beast within would dissolve. He would be her Ragnar again as he searched her out and made love to her to forget as she once had.

$$\Psi$$

IT WASN'T LONG AFTER Ivar was born that Kraka became pregnant again. This time around, the gods were silent in their decree about this son and Bjorn was born, strong, healthy, and fully formed within a year of his brother.

Shortly afterwards followed Hvitserk and then Rognvald. Kraka couldn't believe her luck at all the sons she produced. Ragnar was ecstatic with the babies: fine boys that would grow up and follow in their father's footsteps.

As they grew, Ragnar softened towards Ivar, as if he knew that the child's affliction was somewhat his fault. He took pity on the child, carrying him everywhere and showing him all that his brothers were up to in order to compensate for Ivar's short fallings.

"Look at how strong Ivar is!" Eirik sat down next to Kraka, his bout on the training field over for the moment as Ragnar's younger sons took the helm. Ivar, while boneless in the bottom half of his body, had no qualms about dragging himself through the dirt and onto the training field. Kraka watched as Ivar pulled himself over to a practise sword and grabbed it, waving it around in the way she had seen Ragnar show his siblings.

"I am constantly amazed at that child," Kraka returned, turning as Agnar sat down net to them as well. The animosity he originally displayed towards his stepmother had waned and while they were not as friendly as Kraka was with Eirik, they had started to develop a better relationship. His half-brothers were always a good bridging conversation between them.

"Ivar will become more powerful than the lot of us," Agnar laughed. At his words, Kraka felt a ripple of ice-cold premonition trickle down her spine.

"I believe you are right," she replied. "There is nothing like Ivar's determination to prove himself worthy."

"I totally agree," Eirik chimed in. He leaned across her to grab at a bowl of fruit left for those training. Kraka could smell the heady scent of sweat and that unmistakable smell of maleness. "Ivar is strong, but on top of that, I see him watching us. He will be smarter than all of us as well."

Kraka smiled. She knew Eirik was right and it made her heart swell. She tried to imagine what would have become of her if he had lived. Kraka knew he gave up her kingdom to keep her safe, but would his travels have gotten her to where she now sat, a queen in her own right? She didn't know. Perhaps he would have grown tired of being a beggar on the road and they would have returned to his kingdom and she would be revealed to the world then. Ragnar could have certainly met her if that was the case. However, would he have been as captivated by her if she was of noble standing? For that, she had no answer. All she knew was that if Heimir were to see her now, he would be proud.

"What are you thinking about?" Ragnar had sneaked up on her while she pondered her life and she jumped back, surprised by his presence.

"Oh, old times, Ragnar, before you and before I even knew I could wish for such a happy existence."

Ragnar leaned close, and she kissed him deeply.

CHAPTER 23:

ᕱIRIK

"WHERE ARE WE GOING, BROTHERS?" IVAR SAT atop a wooden board strapped to two poles. Eirik and Agnar were carrying him through the marketplace. Rognvald also tagged along with them, ready to help whenever one of the others tired. When they carried their brother this way the crowd parted to make a path for them. People were fond of the boy and impressed with how much his brothers looked after him and included him in their everyday tasks.

"Agnar and I have a raid to plan," Eirik explained. "We thought you might want to learn about the process."

Ivar was young, but as Ragnar had pointed out to Eirik and Agnar on many occasions, he needed to learn something other than fighting skills. Learning how to raid and plan ahead for things such as battles would help him succeed in their world.

They travelled out of the village and across a small rise until they reached an open stretch that looked down on their town. They set Ivar down and Eirik sat on a rock positioned next to his younger brother. Agnar looked out across the land before he seated himself.

'When will you be raiding Eirik?" Ivar wriggled off the platform and sat in the dirt. His fingers twisted through the dust, making rivers.

"In a few weeks we will set off. We're travelling back to

lands we've already raided. However, Father has not been there for so long, we hope they will not be expecting us and that their security of the area has become lax over the years."

"Tell me," Ivar asked, his hands still working their way through the soil. "What does it feel like to take a life and fight with a sword?"

"Well, you know what it is like to use a sword, out father has already readied you for that," Agnar pointed out. "But, to take a life, well, it is hard the first time. To see the fear on their face and then the nothingness as their life seeps away from them. But, then there is the thrill of the fight, in the midst of all that dying, and you are taken over. It gets into your blood and boils away like one of your mother's stews and you don't think about death anymore but, instead, you crave success more than anything, to make the battle worth it in the end."

"Agnar is right," Rognvald added, pushing his wiry blonde hair out of the way with a thin hand. He was the most reserved of Ragnar's sons, always watching and learning from the world around him. When he spoke, it was to add something important to the conversation rather than merely making conversation. Eirik waited to see what else he would impart. "Killing for the first time is hard, Ivar. If Agnar was truly honest with himself, it never changes, regardless of one death or a hundred. And so, it shouldn't get easier. Each life we take when we go into battle is someone's brother, or son, or father. Always remember that."

Ivar was silent, even his hands had stopped moving. "I want to be able to fight like that. I want to be a greater warrior than even our father." He seemed to ignore all Rognvald said which was typical of Ivar. Where Rognvald had more empathy for his fellow men, Ivar was more interested in becoming a legend. He sought glory and saw nothing else beyond that. Eirik wasn't surprised at this. After all, Ivar had suffered like no one else he had ever known. He probably endured more with his disability on a daily basis than all the men Rognvald had ever killed combined.

Ivar had the potential to be a great leader; he was learning very quickly how the strategy of raids was undertaken. However, it was highly unlikely he would ever participate in battles like his brothers did so Eirik didn't know how to respond to his brother's words.

"Come; let's talk of raiding and what we need to plan. All this talk of Kraka's stew has made me hungry!"

Agnar laughed at him. "For stew or for her?"

Eirik blushed. He knew his feelings for his stepmother were inappropriate. Yet, he could no more stop thinking about her beauty and kindness than stop breathing. Agnar had started teasing him not long after Ivar was born and he had caught Eirik looking at her from afar. Eirik had blushed so deeply that now Agnar teased him about it as often as he could.

"Her stew, brother," Eirik sighed as he turned his head down to the ground, where Ivar had been digging. He dusted it out smooth, so they could draw their battle strategies there.

Kraka filled his mind as he drew out the city boundaries and used rocks as points of interest. She was all Eirik thought about lately. He imagined her talking to him, telling him she was leaving Ragnar because she loved him more. Each night, as he lay down to sleep, this fantasy saw him off to sleep.

Every time she spoke to him, Eirik wished she would tell him that she loved him, only him. At times, he had even suspected she might actually like him more than merely as a stepson. Sometimes, when they accidentally touched hands, or mingled close to each other, Eirik felt the shock of passion between them like the spark of a flame when the fire was first struck. Then, when he made eye contact with her, after those moments, Kraka had reddened slightly and looked away quickly, like she had felt the attraction as well. As if she had instigated it, or returned it.

Eirik knew he was only wishing it, that Kraka loved Ragnar first and foremost. He had seen the way they behaved around each other, after all.

With a deep sigh, Eirik returned, in earnest, to teaching Ivar the art of raiding rather than dwell on his stepmother any longer.

CHAPTER 24:

ḰRAKA

KRAKA REACHED OUT AND STROKED Ragnar's back. They had woken early and made love before it was even light. For today was the day Ragnar would part from her. It was only for a while, but he was setting out with Agnar and Eirik on their first raid of the season. Kraka had wanted to join them; women could after all. However, Ragnar insisted she stay home, with her own boys, for fear that a woman who did not know how to fight would be a risk to them if they came across any trouble. Plus, once more, Kraka was quickening with child. Every sign pointed to now being the wrong time to learn a new skill. Still, she persisted though.

"I wish I could fight like Eirik and Agnar." She was already at it again this morning. Ragnar huffed as he sat up, untangling himself from her naked body. Kraka laid back into the furs. It was off to a bad start. "I miss you when you are gone. And, before long, my boys will be old enough to fight as well and they will leave me too. What will I do then?"

"What the other women do, Kraka," Ragnar replied as he dressed himself. Kraka gazed at him, savouring the last few glimpses of his naked form before he took to the open seas again. "You busy yourself in the ways of the township here. You rule in my stead. Besides, in your condition, there is no need for you to start learning the ways of a shield maiden."

Kraka rubbed her belly, expanding once more with child.

She couldn't believe she was with child once more. After all these years, she thought her childbearing days were over. Ragnar was right; she would be foolish to start training, when she had never even lifted a sword before. But, with each pregnancy, and as her age progressed, she wondered just how much Ragnar still loved her. While he was away, there would always be a trove of younger, prettier women at her husband's disposal. Sure, he still doted on her but, with each baby, her body fell more out of shape. If she was honest with herself, one of the main reasons she wanted to become a warrior had more to do with her physique than her desire to go to war.

"But what if you come across a beautiful peasant girl while you are gone?" She hadn't meant to say it, the words just flowed out of her mouth as her irritation grew. It wasn't that she really wanted to learn how to fight in order to travel with Ragnar, it was that she missed him so terribly while he was gone. She loved this town, yet she still felt like an outsider, even after all these years. While she should have made female friends, she had birthed babies instead—in fact, was still birthing babies—and now the women of her age were not interested in developing friendships with her.

"I will not be coming across any peasant girls!" He was cross; Kraka could see the red filling his face as he clenched his fists. "I will be at sea with Eirik and Agnar and then I will be in Sweden with Eystein."

"Oh course, dear husband," Kraka replied, trying to placate him. "I was only teasing."

Except they both knew she wasn't.

CHAPTER 25:

RAGNAR

"GIVE YOUR REGARDS TO KING EYSTEIN, FOR us!" Eirik called the words out over the water.

Ragnar had travelled with them but now it was time for them to part ways. He waved at his sons and called out that the gods would favour them. "And should we perish, it doesn't matter!" Ragnar added. "We will meet again in Valhalla!" His boys waved back.

"I hear Eystein's daughter is all grown up now," Agnar called out as Ragnar was readying to leave the beach. "I may have to call in and visit on our way back. I am always ready for women once raiding is over and done with!"

Ragnar laughed loudly, the throaty sound revealing his enthusiasm for his son's comments. He waved once more and turned away.

ᛗ

"EYSTEIN! IT'S SO GOOD to see you once more." Ragnar clapped a hand on King Eystein's shoulder. They made this trip every year, taking turns to visit at each other's kingdoms. It had been his turn to visit Eystein when he happened upon Kraka all that time ago.

"Ragnar! Look at you, as ugly as ever, I see." Eystein

laughed and gave Ragnar a bear hug before passing over a cup of ale.

Ragnar always enjoyed his visits to Eystein's kingdom at Uppsala. The area was so different to his own, with their winter being much milder. The terrain was also vastly contrasting. For as long as anyone could remember, people had been buried in this sacred land. In fact, it was here that the mighty gods Odin, Thor, and Freyr were buried. Great mounds over each grave created a strange bumpy landscape. Travelling through the mounds of the gods also brought him closer to them and he bowed his head in reverence. Once past, he looked back and gazed out over the land, smiling widely.

Out in a clearing Ragnar could see Eystein's strange cow, Sibilja. Years prior, when Eystein claimed it would be a battle advantage, Ragnar had laughed at him. Now, news of this strange beast had spread. According to the stories, the animal had a sound so distracting it would set foes against their own side. Ragnar had not seen this in action yet and, if the stories were true, he hoped not to. He shuddered at the thought of a sound being so abrasive that you would slaughter your own men rather than listen to it.

"It almost feels like I am home, King Eystein," he replied to distract himself from the sight of the beast.

"Well, you have visited often enough," Eystein replied, taking Ragnar's arm and leading him to the great hall. "Let's feast!"

RAGNAR WAS DRUNK. HE knew it and everyone else

knew it. Of course, it didn't matter so much because everyone else was as intoxicated as he was. Except for the pretty little thing that was Eystein's daughter, Ingibjorg. Ragnar stared at her now, admiring her cleavage and other womanly curves.

"Aye, she is stunning, is she not?" Rolf spoke as he poured Ragnar another drink.

"She certainly is beautiful," Ragnar reasoned and remember the comment Kraka had made before he left on this journey, the one about him meeting another peasant girl. "Kraka would not be impressed." His words slurred as he spoke, and he hadn't realised he said them aloud until he heard how drunk he was.

"Of course she wouldn't," Rolf replied. "Look at her, beautiful *and* of high standing."

Eystein ambled back to the table then. "Are you eyeing off my daughter, eh?"

"Ragnar was," Rolf said. "We were just comparing her to Kraka."

"That wife of yours is stunning," Eystein conceded. "However, she will never be a match for my daughter. But, I will freely admit I am biased!" He laughed and motioned to a slave to pour him another drink.

Ragnar sat there, drunk and concerned that he was nothing more than a joke to those around him. Kraka had been a good wife, he had always known that. Peasants knew how to work hard and love the simple things in life. He had fallen for her wit and beauty, but he also knew that she would be a valuable asset as his wife. She would not take advantage of him as noble women might, since they were used to climbing social ladders at whatever cost it required.

He looked at Rolf, who was now talking to one of

Eystein's men. Over the years, Rolf had always suggested Kraka was not the right woman for him, and not socially equipped to be a queen of such a vast kingdom. Ragnar usually brushed his comments off, laughing at him and moving the conversation away from that topic.

But, he had heard the whispers, those who thought like Rolf did. Yet, Kraka could not be faulted as a queen. While she should have been overwhelmed at the start, being introduced to such a vast community, becoming pregnant with their first heir, and having to learn how to be a ruler, she hadn't stumbled. Although, she asked many questions, she only had to ask each one once. She never forgot anything told to her about how to be a queen. In fact, Ragnar had sometimes caught himself staring at her in awe, as she intrinsically seemed to know how to handle situations. If Ragnar had been an outsider, looking in on Kraka, he would have thought she was born of high standing. Her name and the common gossip chain the only indicators she was anything less than royalty.

ᛘ

THE NEXT DAY, RAGNAR and Eystein went hunting. As they tracked animals, they talked of their enduring friendship. Their tie was an unusual one among their kind. Normally conflict arose—usually ambition in some form or another—and tore apart kingly ties. However, Ragnar and Eystein had managed to remain friends their entire lives.

"How many years have you and Eystein been visiting?" Rolf asked as they broke for a meal.

"I am not sure," Eystein replied. "Ingibjorg was not born.

In fact, I don't think I was even married yet when we first gathered."

"It was the year before you married," Ragnar replied. "By the second year, I had to make my first trip here because your wife would not allow you to leave her so soon."

"Ah, that's right!" Eystein chuckled. The year after that, I returned from my trip to your lands to find out Ingibjorg had been born. My, she was a pretty baby."

"She still is," Rolf replied. "If you don't mind me saying so out of line."

"No, of course not." The king laughed again.

"If I were of a higher standing, I would try my hand at catching her. Although, with Ragnar around, he is always poaching the best women, isn't that right, Leif?"

Leif nodded. "Yes, I will never forgive him for stealing Kraka right out from under my nose." Leif laughed, but Ragnar looked fiercely at him then. Had he really stolen Kraka away from Leif? He couldn't remember his wife ever saying something like that. Although, would she, considering Leif was one of Ragnar's men?

"Yes, Ragnar gets all of the women, that's for sure," Eystein joined in. "Remember that time, when we were in Denmark and encountered that lady, what was her name?" Eystein fished for a name.

"Hilde?" Ragnar asked.

"Yes! That was her! Hilde. She was a fine whore, wasn't she? Both of us couldn't keep our eyes off her, yet, we all know who she picked, don't we?"

Everyone laughed. Ragnar blushed. He didn't like this talk of his way with women. He knew women liked to follow him, but he didn't like when it was mentioned out loud.

"Right, then," Ragnar said, as he stood up. "I think it is

time for a visit to the woods."

He walked away, leaving the men behind, laughing at him.

When he returned, he entered the conversation to discover they were still talking about him and Kraka.

"I agree, he should have picked someone else," Rolf said as he took another long sip of ale. "Someone like your daughter, Eystein. She is of a noble enough standing for Ragnar. In fact, why has that never happened? It would secure the bond between your two kingdoms nicely."

Ragnar sat down and Rolf leaned over to him, putting an arm over his shoulder and pulling him in.

"It would be an honour to have Ragnar marry my Ingibjorg, that is true," Eystein replied, joining in with Rolf's banter. "In fact, why haven't we done that yet, Ragnar? I think I'm offended that you never considered my daughter."

Except they had, Eystein was just too drunk to remember. Years ago, they talked about this very subject. They had decided that Ragnar saw Ingibjorg more as a child of his or a sister rather than a mate. He had seen her from birth and it just didn't seem right. However, as the room spiralled down, once more, into drunken abandonment, it seemed like Ingibjorg was back on the negotiation table.

"You should put away Kraka," Rolf insisted. "She is just a peasant anyway, and take up Ingibjorg as your new wife."

Eystein agreed. In fact, everyone agreed with Rolf, and, by the end of the hunting trip, Ragnar had somehow wound up betrothed to Ingibjorg. He was horrified. As he lay down to sleep, the world spinning from the change in his life as much as from the ale he had consumed, Ragnar wondered how he was going to fix this great mess.

Perhaps they will all forget on the morrow, he told himself repeatedly as the world slowed and he slipped away into slumber. After all, they were very drunk. What was the likelihood of them remembering this tomorrow?

In the morning, however, he was still betrothed to Ingibjorg.

CHAPTER 26:

ℜAGNAR

"WE NEED TO STOP HERE," RAGNAR SAID AS they reached a calm cove. His men didn't question him, but busied themselves with slowing the ship and bringing it into shore.

After they were on land, Ragnar gathered all the men about him. He had thought long and hard after his betrothal and he still didn't know what to do about the mess. Ragnar loved Kraka, even after all these years. She had been a good wife and an excellent queen. There was no way he wanted to repay her service and love by putting her out on the street.

Yet, he couldn't break it off with Ingibjorg either. Somehow, the jesting about Ragnar and her had gone from simple fun and been goaded into a fully-fledged betrothal that was now bound between both parties.

He had wound up in a mess of epic proportions. Ragnar stared at his men, looking them each squarely in the eye as his did his round. He stopped on Rolf last; still disgusted at the man for airing his true feelings about Kraka and her peasant roots and getting him stuck so fast like this.

"We are nearly home. As you all now know, I have wound up betrothed to Eystein's daughter, Ingibjorg. It was not of my doing, yet, I cannot get out of the predicament now without offending King Eystein." Ragnar still maintained eye contact with Rolf. "Luckily, the betrothal will be a long one, because of Ingibjorg's age. So, as a result of this, I do not want a single word spoken about it, not to each other and most certainly not to my queen, Kraka. If I hear that any of you have done so, I will kill you. Do I make myself clear?"

Ragnar watched Erik swallow, pleased at the man's discomfort. However, it was nothing compared to the pain and discomfort Ragnar was now feeling. The other men nodded and grunted their replies. The king turned, startling a trio of birds in the trees next to the beach and he stormed back towards the boat. His men scuttled along behind him.

Once back on board, they set sail once more. Ragnar knew they would be home soon, even as early as that evening. He was excited to return, the ache for his wife nearly quenched. However, he also worried that somehow Kraka would know. She had a gift, one that Ragnar rarely doubted. Yet, with all his heart, he hoped she would not guess this new situation.

Ragnar spoke to no one on that journey home. Instead, he watched the horizon and wondered just how he was ever going to break the news to Kraka.

CHAPTER 27:

ᚱRAKA

KRAKA ENTERED THE WELCOME FEAST WITH trepidation. She knew her life was about to change. It was not what she expected, of that she was sure. However, it had become known to her that Ragnar had done something horrible. Something he couldn't get out of.

She held her head high as her gaze swept the room. Kraka could see Ragnar, sitting at the other end. He was watching her but she didn't give him her attention. Instead, she stopped along the way from the entrance to their chairs, greeting people who had returned and chatting to women about whatever they fancied. She took her time, not even glancing at Ragnar. Finally, she reached their platform and stood before her husband.

"Welcome home, King Ragnar," she said with a smile. It was likely insincere, or it felt like it on the inside. However, externally, she was sure no one except for maybe her husband would notice.

"Kraka!" Ragnar jumped up, his arms stretched out wide. He stepped forward and embraced her. She felt his strong arms envelope her, the familiar shape of them. They always brought her comfort. Or, they had in the past. Kraka inhaled deeply. She could smell the sweat of him along with his own personal aroma, the one that made her insides squirm in delight even as she closed her eyes and tried not to cry. "I have missed you so."

"Oh, how I have missed you, Ragnar," Kraka returned. She was honest in her words though, unlike the lies that unwound from her husband. She unravelled herself from his embrace and sat down in her chair. "Please, what news do you bring back with you from Sweden?"

It was a loaded question. She knew what the news was; she just wanted Ragnar to admit it freely, here in the room full of people. Kraka turned to her husband, the smile from earlier returning to her face. Ragnar looked at her, but refused to make eye contact. Instead, he seemed suddenly fascinated with her left cheek.

"Eystein is well, his family is well. Our visit went as it usually does, dear wife."

Kraka maintained her gaze. Her smile, however, slipped slightly. She wanted to ask him again, yet she found her mouth would not open and the words wouldn't come. Turning back to the crowd, she felt her tension ease. "Well, then all is as it should be, it seems."

$$\Psi$$

LATER, WHEN THE FEAST was over and Ragnar and Kraka had retired for the night, she decided it was time to tackle the subject once more. Kraka waited until she was settled comfortably in their bed. Ragnar was sitting as he fiddled with his boots, untying them and starting to pull them off.

"So, Ragnar, surely there is some news you bring me from Sweden?"

Ragnar paused in his task, his boot still half off his foot.

His shoulders had hitched up a little as he turned and gazed at her. It was a slow, deliberate movement.

"As I said earlier, there is no news." He turned away from her after speaking, returning, instead, to the task of removing his shoes.

"Really, husband? There is nothing you have to say about your visit to King Eystein's?"

He didn't turn this time. Kraka craned her neck a little, trying to see what was going on with Ragnar's face. She couldn't see anything, but his shoulders tightened up even more before he spoke again.

"I am tired, Kraka, can we just do away with the talk of Sweden tonight?" Ragnar pulled his second boot off in a flurry of hastened activity and dove under the covers with her. He lay on his back, his eyes closed, as if that would be enough to fall asleep and stop Kraka from her obvious onslaught.

"Well, if you are so tired, why not rest your eyes while I tell you of the news I have received coming out of Sweden." Ragnar visibly stiffened. His eyes still remained closed though. "It has come to my attention that my husband has found himself betrothed to another woman. In my humble opinion, that is news."

Ragnar was wide awake now and starring at her like a trapped animal.

"Who told you that?" His voice was hollow, shadowed with fear.

"Oh, don't worry, none of your men need lose their life. Three little birds that followed your journey returned to me this morning with the news."

Kraka watched Ragnar intently. He looked like he was going to be sick, the colour had bleached out of his face. She was so angry with him she wanted to pommel his chest with her fists and tell him she hated him for what he was about to do to her. But then, she saw tears seeping from the corners of his eyes. She paused, her fists still wound and ready for action.

"I didn't want this, Kraka," Ragnar said quietly, the words sneaking out like a secret he had tried to contain but no longer could. "Somehow they all forced me into it and now I am trapped."

"Then don't do it," Kraka replied, practically. "You are already married. Surely Eystein can see reason within that?"

"If you were of an equal standing of Ingibjorg, then yes, he would." His words lingered, frosty, in the air between them and Kraka gasped.

It was time for the truth.

After all these years, she knew now was the right time to expose herself. Kraka rubbed her belly, the baby within kicking out against her inner turmoil.

"I am of equal standing to Ingibjorg," Kraka replied, quietly.

She turned her eyes upwards, away from her burgeoning belly and sought out Ragnar. He stared back at her, a mixture of emotions on his face. Mostly, however, disbelief showed.

"Only by marriage, Kraka," Ragnar said. "I wish it were different."

"No, not by marriage." A small bloom of anger now tainted her words. A fire was smouldering inside of her and she was ready to feed it. "My birthright is not what you think it is. Grima and Aki were not my parents, but my foster parents. They only gained that title because they killed my true foster father, Heimir."

There was a flicker of recognition in Ragnar's face with

the mention of Heimir, so Kraka continued with her story.

At first Ragnar didn't seem to believe what she said. To give him credit, it was a fanciful tale that anyone could tell. After all, when her parents, Sigurd and Brynhildr died, Aslaug and Heimir had never been seen again. People had always gossiped about the outcome, but there was never any proof to suggest either had survived. In reality, anyone could step forward and claim they were Aslaug or Heimir. What she needed to give Ragnar was proof. She gazed down at her stomach once more, her hands cupped gently around its precious cargo.

"I know you think this story is not true," Kraka said. "But, I will offer you this, if I am truly the daughter of Sigurd and Brynhildr, then this baby will be born with the image of a snake in his eye, a representation of the serpent his grandfather once slayed. If you can wait as long as it takes to birth this child, then you will see. If the he is born without this sign, then you are free to leave me and to marry Ingibjorg. I just ask that you have the patience to wait that long."

For the first time since Ragnar had returned home from Sweden, Kraka could see the tension bleed out of his shoulders. She had given him a reason to hold off for a moment.

Kraka had given him an escape route, regardless of the outcome.

CHAPTER 28:

ℜAGNAR

RAGNAR PACED THE LENGTH OF THE GREAT hall. Kraka was in labour; their baby was being born. By the end of this long night, it was likely Ragnar would know his new destiny.

While he trusted the fateful prophecies of Kraka, this time he was unsure. Her story seemed so contrived, so desperate in an effort to keep their marriage. It was so conveniently timed to help her in her cause, that Ragnar doubted the truth behind it. He could understand her need to make him believe though. If he were Kraka, he certainly wouldn't want to return to a life of servitude after the way she had lived all these years.

He had kept his word, as had his men about the betrothal to Ingibjorg, so there was no expectation yet that Ragnar would put Kraka aside. At least he had that on his side. However, he was saddened by the prospect of having to marry Eystein's daughter. Ingibjorg was beautiful, but she wasn't Kraka. She would never be Kraka.

Yet, he didn't know just how he was supposed to get out the mess of the situation. He didn't want to marry Eystein's daughter, but he didn't want to offend her either. More importantly, he didn't want to upset the longstanding relationship her had with her father.

It had been three weeks since Ragnar returned from

Sweden and Kraka told him about her lineage. Ragnar hoped with all his heart that her words would turn out to be true, even if it meant war when he broke off the betrothal with Ingibjorg. He loved Kraka, whoever she was. He couldn't care less if she was from the Volsung line or if she really was just the peasant child of Grima and Aki. However, if she really were Sigurd and Brynhildr's child, then Ragnar would be free of the all the antagonism he had received as a result of him marrying so far below his own standing. It would be a welcome relief.

"Ragnar." It was one of Kraka's attendants. Ragnar turned, awaiting the answer that would change his world, one way or another.

The woman reached forward, handing Ragnar the bundle that was his destiny. Ragnar accepted the small squirming child. Kraka had given him the entirety of free will in regard to his decision by presenting their baby to him. He could reject this child, turn away and dismiss their marriage, claiming Kraka's story was untrue. Or, he could accept this child as his own and bring war down on them by way of Sweden.

Ragnar looked down at the small, helpless child, the one whose life he could keep or quell. The blood of birth was still evident, but, more importantly, the child's eyes were open, for all the world to see.

And, what Ragnar saw amazed him.

"THIS CHILD WILL BE called, Sigurd, just like his grandfather!" Ragnar roared it out across the great hall. His wife was seated beside him, exhaustion present on her face. However, she told him she wouldn't miss this event for anything.

Aslaug.

His wife's name was Aslaug.

He still couldn't believe it. After all those weeks of worry, Ragnar couldn't even care that they were about to become fierce enemies with the one country he never imagined he would. Instead, he stared at his wife, the woman he loved just as much as he had his other wife, Thora, and thanked the gods for blessing him so.

People had not believed the story when Ragnar first told it to them, explaining Aslaug's lineage and how she was as dignified and of as high a standing as he was. But, if the king said it was so, eventually, people had to believe it.

However, it was telling his men—those that had been bound to secrecy about the upcoming marriage to Ingibjorg—that brought Ragnar the most joy. He was able to look at Rolf and Leif and tell them just how important his queen really was and how huge a mistake they had made on her behalf. It was like watching an event unfold that someone had sworn would not occur but had anyway, against all of the odds.

Ragnar smirked as he told them. Rolf looked horrified, and Ragnar wondered if he worried about his fate as a result of the news. Although, Ragnar knew Rolf was too good a warrior to warrant letting him go, or even killing him outright. Leif was contrite, looking down, looking across the hall, looking anywhere but at his king.

He was relieved more than anything when it came to the birth of Sigurd. While Ragnar would have to worry about the consequences of the news heading towards Sweden, he was happy to know that his family would stay the same.

With the birth of Aslaug from the peasant girl, Kraka, people would create new tales, no longer about the king and the peasant. Instead, people would talk of how the king had always known his farmer girl was more than she presented to the world. There would be those who commented about how Aslaug had always seemed more regal than her upbringing had expected. And, how some people had just *known* she was more important than a peasant girl could ever be.

Ragnar smiled at the prospect of this.

CHAPTER 29:

ASLAUG

"PLEASE, KEEP YOURSELF SAFE, MY SONS TO another woman," Aslaug was sad to see Eirik and Agnar head off into such a volatile situation. She wanted to cry, could feel the hot sting of unshed tears fighting for release behind her eyes. Yet she held them there, trapped away for only her to know about. Aslaug did not want the people around her to see just how much she fretted over her stepsons having to deal with the situation in Sweden.

She leaned over and hugged Agnar. The embrace was quick, their relationship still having some distance between them. Kraka cared deeply for Agnar. Yet, she held him back, knowing Agnar was friendly towards her but still felt he was somehow betraying his mother if he allowed himself get to close to Kraka.

When it came to Eirik, however, she let her hug linger. She held him tight and felt his strong arms around her, hugging her fiercely back. He hung to her, as if he never wanted to let her go and she relished the embrace.

Ragnar stepped forward. Aslaug could feel him there, at her side, his heat reaching out to her, reminding her that she held his son, even though their arms felt the same around her. She wondered if Eirik kissed in the same way his father did, if his hands would be as gentle on her body.

She stepped back then, as those inappropriate ideas

entered her mind. These were not thoughts to be had about her stepson, not when her husband stood next to her. In fact, not ever.

She smiled quickly at Eirik and their eyes met. He knew. She could tell from the way he blushed that Eirik somehow knew what she was thinking. Or, perhaps, he had been thinking along similar lines. Kraka had always suspected Eirik held stronger feelings for her than he should for his stepmother. Now she knew without question that Eirik wanted her in the same way that Ragnar had her.

"I will miss you, my shining boys." Ragnar's voice was thick with unshed emotion. Aslaug knew he was proud of his sons and wished them all the success in the world. However, there was always the mixed emotion of a parting such as this because men always hankered for Valhalla. Ragnar needed to be happy if this were to happen. Yet, he was conflicted, she suspected. After all, she did not want to see Agnar or Eirik die at such a young age, and she was only their stepmother. Kraka wanted them here in the present for as long as possible, even if they sought an honourable death that would take them away to the otherworld and Odin's famed halls of Valhalla.

"We shall return, victorious," Agnar replied and Aslaug felt a shudder of premonition. She brushed it aside, figuring if she didn't dwell on it, there would be no time for it to develop into an outcome. Instead, she concentrated her energies on a valiant result, one that would see the relationship between Eystein and Ragnar restored.

"Yes," Eirik responded. "We shall make Eystein understand about our good queen and stepmother. This mess will be sorted—one way or another."

Eirik stared at Aslaug. She could see the words not spoken

as they threatened to pour from his mouth.

"Well, you boys need to be on your way. Victory comes to those who embrace it, not to those who linger on the shorelines and say goodbye to their families for too long. Step forward now and welcome your destiny." Aslaug stepped back, away from Ragnar's sons, allowing them the space they needed to escape. She hoped Eirik would take the cue and leave, taking his unshed words along with him.

As she stepped back out of the way, a piercing scream was heard. Before she could even look in the direction it came from, the noise was silenced. The bustle of the crowd filled its place, though, and swiftly news travelled through the gathering.

"Trygve is dead!" Aslaug heard it repeated over and over again. She rushed forward as she saw the man's mother falling over his body. Men around them hurried to heft the massive log off the body. The same log used only moments earlier to lower Eirik and Agnar's last longship into the water. Aslaug knelt beside Trygve's mother, placing her arms around the distraught woman's shoulders.

Ragnar was beside her, dragging Trygve out from under the log. Leif helped him and they lifted the man high before rushing him through the crowd. Aslaug and the man's mother, Solveig, followed closely behind. The woman sobbed and howled so Aslaug had to lead the way.

"Trygve!" Solveig screamed her son's name out as she entered the main hall.

Aslaug stepped back, colliding with Eirik as she did so. He embraced her and she folded into his arms, burying her head from the sight of the distraught mother. Carefully, he lowered her down onto a bench. She still cowered within his arms.

"This is such a bad omen," she whispered into his

shoulder, not even realising she was speaking aloud. "Dear gods, please don't let anything happen to my boys."

"We will be fine," Eirik replied. She gazed up at him and he smiled at her. Reaching down, he kissed the top of her head and she closed her eyes as his lips lingered in her hair. For a moment, it was as if Ragnar was here comforting her.

Starting, she opened her eyes and pulled back from her stepson. Eirik looked at her, his gaze impenetrable and Aslaug found she couldn't look away. The sound of grief faded away and she became trapped in a world where only Eirik existed.

Eirik bent forward again, his eyes closing as his lips sought her own. The unexplainable pull she always had with her stepson intensified as she felt her own eyes closing. Her hand reached up between them, the final response before she did something she truly regretted. "We can't do this."

Eirik was silent. His eyes were open now and Aslaug wondered if he would try to deny what had just nearly happened.

"Why not?"

Aslaug gasped. However, before she could answer, Solveig was between them.

"This is all your fault!" the woman screamed, her bony finger poking Aslaug hard in the chest. "You should have just let Ragnar marry Ingibjorg. May the gods curse you for the death of my son!"

Eirik rose to his feet as Ragnar strode across the room and grabbed the woman.

"That's not true," Eirik shouted.

However, Aslaug suspected it was all her fault.

Ψ

"I FEAR FOR YOUR boys," Aslaug admitted as they stood on the shore, watching Eirik and Agnar's small fleet disappear on the horizon. "Especially since that boy died as they set sail. It is a bad omen. And now you have to set sail as well, off on your own meeting."

"Do not fear for them, dear wife. Please, forget everything Solveig said to you as that was only her grief talking. Perhaps it was a sacrifice the gods required to keep them safe on this journey," Ragnar responded. "They have their destiny to uphold. So, do I. This meeting is important; the other earls in the area need to know what King Eystein has done so they can be prepared. If all goes well, we will have many on our side should this meeting between my sons and Eystein goes sour."

"I know, and it is not for me to say what the gods have in store for them," she replied as they turned. The ships were now too small for them to see that far out to sea. She reached for Ragnar's arm, hooking her own through his as they walked. "However, I somehow feel this mess is all my fault. I should have told you about Grima and Aki before now."

"Why didn't you tell me earlier?" Ragnar stopped. He turned and his questioning gaze bore into her.

"I wanted my foster parents to suffer in the same way I had suffered every day I was with them. I hoped that the longer they lived, the more they would come to understand that what they had done to me—and to Heimir—was wrong. Plus, I wanted to know that you loved me for myself, and not for my standing. It was selfish of me, on both counts, and now your boys must sort it all out for me."

Aslaug's gaze dropped, she could no longer look at her husband. She hoped his sons would be safe, even more now that she had articulated her circumstances.

Ragnar put his arm around her shoulders and pulled her in close. "I have always loved you; you should have no doubt of that, Aslaug. I knew from the very moment I laid eyes on you that you were meant for me alone. But, even if you didn't know that, know that I hold no bad feelings towards you if this situation gets too far out of hand." Aslaug sobbed. It was a dry heave that threatened to open up the vast swell of tears behind her eyes.

"I don't deserve you, Ragnar."

CHAPTER 30:

ℭIRIK

"CHARGE!"

Negotiations with King Eystein had fallen through. Agnar and Eirik had anticipated this. As a result, they were now at war.

Eirik surged forward, his brother at his side. Running through the field, they held their axes at the ready and shields out in front. They were close enough to see the faces of the men on Eystein's side.

The sound of men and shields and metal clashing was always something to which Eirik could never adjust. A grinding, twisting sound clattered across the landscape with an echo of weapons singing as they collided. This was invariably mixed with the dull thud of metal and flesh. In turn, they mingled with those human sounds that should have been louder: the gurgles and grunts as men were injured and died. Finally, over all of this, was the battle cry of those not yet injured.

"Eystein's group is not large," Agnar shouted across to Eirik, who grunted in reply. He was involved with decapitating one of the king's men at that point in time and hadn't had a chance to fully assess the situation at hand.

"His numbers might be comparable to ours, but that doesn't mean we should be lax, Agnar," Eirik finally returned once he had stepped back a little and glanced quickly around.

He felt newly hopeful at the outcome. Ever since Trygve had died while they were moving out the fleet, Eirik had been unnerved. His moment with Aslaug after that, a further indication that he could expect troubled times ahead. Eirik tried not to think of that last moment shared with Aslaug, of how she had looked at him as he had seen her look at his father.

A horn blared, off to one side and Eirik was actually relieved with the distraction. He and his brother turned at the sound and saw that many more of Eystein's troops now descended on them. The pair shot worried looks to each other. They had been too presumptuous.

"This will not be an easy feat," Eirik called back. It was Agnar's turn not to respond, as he was heavily involved in the new group of troops. While Eirik slew his way through the Eystein's initial troops, Agnar took possession of half of their own men to try to secure a foothold with the second of Eystein's groups.

During this time, Eirik was distracted by a strange sound in the distance.

He knew immediately what it was: Eystein's battle cow, Sibilja. Eirik had heard his father tell stories about Eystein's cow and the strange effect its cry had on those in battle. In response, he clenched his jaw tightly as if that would help block out the sound of Sibilja's bellowing wail.

It could be heard relentlessly at the front of the line. He watched as some of his men fell back, the noise not only spooking them but also confusing them, bewitched as they were by the cow's power.

Agnar called out to Eirik and he turned, distracted. His brother was standing still, covering his ears and watching as his group turned on each other, or tried to whip the air with their weapons instead of the enemy. Already, Sibilja was winning Eystein's battle.

Eirik gritted his teeth and fought the urge to allow the cow's keening cry wash over him, to envelop him and consume him until he became a puppet of the animal, rather than the other way around. He wept with the struggle, his teeth grinding together until he could spit out tiny little slivers of his own broken teeth.

"Agnar!" Eirik called out his brother's name only as a reference point for his own struggle. He did not know if Agnar heard him at all, so he turned.

He watched as one of his own men, who were waving his arms around in a frenzied manner, knocked down his brother. An arc of dark blood sprayed through the air, covering the very man who had killed Agnar.

Eirik dropped to his knees. He called out his brother's name, roared it out until his voice was hoarse and his throat felt like it was raw and on fire. Turning, everywhere Eirik could see the destruction of his men, of Ragnar's army. The men fought imaginary foes, or turned on themselves and slashed their arms and legs rather than listen to the horrendous cries coming from Sibilja. All Eirik could see was the constant splash of red as his army appeared to implode. He dropped his head and covered his ears, waiting for it all to be over so he could join his brother in Valhalla.

But, death did not come to Eirik then.

Instead, King Eystein appeared.

"Sibilja!" The king's voice boomed over the clatter of the battlefield. The cow went silent and the clatter of noise instantly ceased. A moment or two later, as those who remained looked around them and saw what they had done, created a new noise. It was a strange, defeated sound, as if regret was suddenly vocalised here on the battlefield for just one brief moment in time. As soon as the noise started, it began to taper off, dying down and dissipating into the air like fog as the sun warmed it.

Eirik raised his eyes until he could lock his gaze on Eystein. The man approached, striding through the mud, and blood, and gore of the field until he was directly in front of Eirik. Still, Eirik maintained eye contact. He would not blink, break his gaze, or look away, for fear of looking weak.

Of course, he was weak, though. His whole army had been defeated by the bellow of a cow. For a moment, he remembered the woman, Solveig, who had cursed Aslaug and wondered if this would be how it would end. And, if Aslaug would miss him after he died.

"I have a proposition for you, Eirik, son of Ragnar." King Eystein reached out a hand, to help Eirik up, but he refused. Instead, he staggered to his feet, not ready for help from Eystein. Not now, and not ever.

"I do not care to hear it, Eystein. You have decimated my army, and why? Because you fancied marrying your daughter off to my father—your friend—even though he was already married."

With huge self-restraint, Eirik resisted spitting at the man. "Your father practically begged for my daughter."

Eirik laughed at Eystein but it was a strange hacking sound that was filled with the bitterness he felt towards the situation created by this man.

"You and my father have been friends for so long, and yet you want to sully your relationship with nothing more than lies. I know very well that my father was coerced into this betrothal," Eirik laughed. "Perhaps," Eystein finally conceded. "However, I think this can still be rectified."

Eirik looked at Eystein, his curiosity piqued. "I cannot see how this mess could possibly be fixed now."

"You could marry my daughter," Eystein finally said. "All would be forgiven then."

It was difficult to know the right response to the king's proposition. Marrying Ingibjorg would be the better option. They were much closer in age and it was more fitting than giving the girl off to someone as old as her own father.

However, all Eirik could see in his mind's eye was Aslaug. He pictured her as he had left her, sad, beautiful, and regretful. Always he had wondered just how much she really cared for him. But, now he knew. She had wanted to kiss him as much as he did. It was only her honour to his father that caused her to push him away; of this, he had no doubt.

While he knew nothing could ever eventuate between himself and Aslaug, Eirik knew he would regret everything about this whole sorry mess if he relented to marrying Ingibjorg. How could he marry someone for whom he had no real feelings? What sort of relationship would that result in?

Finally, Eirik thought of his father. He loved Ragnar, as a son should. However, a small part of him resented his father for the present mess, and also for being married to someone like Aslaug. A woman who looked at him as if he was the centre of her universe, Eirik had never had that. The closest he had ever gotten to that was the love of his brother, Agnar, or of his own sweet mother. Both of those people were dead and here was Eirik, standing in a field and deciding the fate of his family.

He could do it; he could marry Ingibjorg. The girl was beautiful after all, and that would go a long way if her personality turned out to be lacking. They could make a life together as well as keep Eystein and Ragnar on civil terms.

However, would they ever really be on civil terms after something like this? Always, the initial dilemma would continue to simmer away under the surface until further conflict arose.

Eirik squared his shoulders and gave his answer.

"No, I will not marry your daughter, Eystein." He said it firmly. There was not a shadow of doubt present as he stood there and stared the man down. "You can kill me now, do what you please with my own body, but I ask that Agnar is returned home to Ragnar. The few men that still stand need safe passage as well. I ask sincerely that you grant this wish."

Eystein stared earnestly at Eirik, assessing him before replying. "As you wish, Eirik."

King Eystein allowed Eirik's men to take up the body of Agnar and return safely to their waiting ships. As soon as the fleet left the shore, Eirik stepped forward, waiting for death to greet him.

The last thing Eirik saw was the sweet memory of a woman he could never have.

CHAPTER 31:

ASLAUG

ASLAUG GASPED WHEN LEIF ENTERED THE room. His clothing was torn and patched up as if he was in a great hurry. His face bore the brunt of many bruises and he limped when as he approached her.

"You have news about Eirik and Agnar?" The words were whispered, as if she didn't want to give them too much substance, like this would make the words and Leif's answer more importance. As if mere words had a life of their own in situations like this. She leaned forward in her chair, her hands grasping tightly to the armrests, her body hummed with anticipation.

"I have news, Queen Aslaug. Is the king present today?"

Leif was stalling and Aslaug knew it. She knew what that likely meant, too.

"King Ragnar is still away with his meeting of kings and earls. However, you can tell me what has happened in Sweden between my stepsons and King Eystein."

"Agnar perished during the battle."

Aslaug sagged into her chair. "But Eirik is alright?" She had hope; it rose in her like the bloom of sap in the trees in springtime. She smiled; ready to learn about how Eirik had made Eystein succumb.

"Eirik is also dead," Leif returned. "King Eystein offered his daughter in marriage to him, but Eirik refused the offer."

Aslaug felt the world drop out from under her feet. The walls felt as if they were closing in on her and tip on an angle as she tried to comprehend the words being uttered to her. Eirik was not dead. He couldn't be. Not Ragnar's shining son, the one that looked so much like his father, the one that made her own heart confused and sing for him in the same way it did for his father.

She could hear the whispers of voices coming from so far away that she suspected they were in another longhouse. Yet, when she looked around the room, she could see Leif's lips moving. More horrible words were spewing from them, no doubt.

The world waivered, blurred, and turned red with the desolation and fury she felt consuming her. Wiping at her eyes, she held up her hand and saw she wept tears of blood for Eirik.

Before Aslaug could even catch her breath, or wipe her emotion off her face, her true sons walked in. They had been away as well, although their mission was a simple raid. She looked up, and counted their heads, trying to work out if they had brought good news or bad. Even before Ivar opened his mouth, Aslaug knew that Rognvald was not there. She clasped her hands together, wringing them until they twisted so hard together, it was hard to tell where one hand ended and the other started.

"Where is Rognvald?" Aslaug was sick of bad news. However, she needed to know immediately just how horrible it was to be.

Ivar had been carried in on his usual pole and panel device. He was deposited on the ground next to Aslaug. Her son reached forward and untangled her hands, delaying his words. His blue eyes looked up at her. Ragnar's eyes.

"Rognvald did not survive."

Aslaug thought she was ready for the blow but Ivar's words assaulted her. She was numb by the end of his sentence, her tears now dried up and gone. Aslaug had no idea how to react to this news, her mind seemed preoccupied with the previous announcement, and there was no room for her to even grieve her own son at this point. Instead, the words tumbled out. Rote, ones she had heard said by every mother who had ever lost a son in battle.

"My son is with Odin now; there is no greater glory for him."

$$\Psi$$

"WE NEED TO AVENGE Eirik and Agnar," Aslaug said even though it pained her to say Eirik's name. "Your stepbrothers were great warriors and you should not tolerate such a thing as what King Eystein has done to them, especially considering the reason behind their death. It is not like Rognvald's death," She paused, another name that brought her great pain to say aloud. She took a deep breath before continuing. "Rognvald went raiding so his death was a consequence of that. Eirik and Agnar, on the other hand, went to fix a problem that was caused by King Eystein initially. They should not have lost their lives for that man's faults. I will assist you all in whatever you need in this task."

Aslaug sat next to young Sigurd and her hand absently reached out and brushed her son's hair out of his eyes while she waited for Ivar's response. The boy wriggled his way out of her clutches.

Ivar looked at his mother. "I will not go to Sweden."

His words were abrupt and so sudden that Aslaug gasped at the shock of his refusal. She couldn't understand it. Out of all her sons, Ivar was always the one who was the most eager to go to war.

"But, if something were to have happen to you, Ivar, and your brothers were still alive, I am sure they would step in to do what is right," Aslaug replied.

"There is too much sorcery afoot here. King Eystein has that cow of his and it would only lead to our deaths as well. And then, what would you do? Sigurd is too young and our father would have to find others to fight on our behalf."

Ivar spoke reason. However, it didn't mean Aslaug had to agree with it. "Then how can we do this, Ivar?" There had to be a way. Her stepsons had to be avenged along with her own dignity. Ragnar had said he would not hold anything against her for the loss of his sons over this. But, when he found out he had actually lost two of them to save her honour, things might be different.

"Sibilja is so powerful that her very bellowing brings much calamity to those around it. I would imagine that Agnar and Eirik had this happen to them. They were aware of Sibilja's power, but I suspect they thought her sound could be overcome. I do not want to risk my own men against this sort of a weapon."

Sigurd spoke up next. He may have been too young to fight yet but, like his father, he was wise and could counsel sagely even though he had not lived through many years.

"I can see King Eystein falling." Aslaug looked at her son while he spoke. She could see the snake dancing in his eye and she knew he now spoke the truth. "It will take three days, but we must prepare ourselves to attack the king. Regardless of the wealth he holds, his position at Uppsala is precarious now that he has fought back against the mighty Ragnar Lodbrok."

Sigurd looked around at all of his brothers. Aslaug held her breath. His words seemed to spurn on his siblings to side with him and against Ivar but she couldn't be sure, until they spoke, where their loyalties would fall.

"Perhaps we should think this through a little more, Ivar," said Hviserk. "I am sure, between all of us, we can come up with a plan to defeat King Eystein."

A sigh escaped her lips. She swallowed it quickly, hoping no one would notice. Aslaug sat back, watching as her sons started to throw ideas back and forth, the fire of Sigurd's words motivating them more than revenge at the moment. It didn't matter to Aslaug though, she was just glad that Sigurd could help change their minds so easily. It helped that they knew Sigurd was like her and could see things that others couldn't.

In the end, Ivar did come around and declared they must seek vengeance for the unjust deaths of their half-brothers.

Ψ

RAGNAR HAD STILL NOT returned from his meeting of kings by the time a fleet to attack King Eystein was ready. Unable to wait any longer, Aslaug's sons set out on their quest for vengeance. Aslaug insisted she travel with them and help defend Eirik and Agnar's honour. Ivar had been against this but she prevailed, telling him that she knew more than he did about how they must defeat King Eystein. Ivar, knowing his mother's propensity for perception when all reasonable avenues were exhausted, relented, and put her in charge of the land troops.

When they arrived in Sweden, it was decided they must put as much fear into King Eystein as possible, so they killed those that stood in their way. From the very moment they alighted onto the shores of Sweden, Ivar commanded that everyone in sight must be killed. He had no sympathy and his army followed suit under his and Aslaug's instruction. She believed in her son and knew it had to be done to make things right again.

Ivar was relentless in every village they passed through. Initially, he may have been lax to join the cause for his stepbrothers but now that he was in favour of their revenge, he didn't approach anything half-heartedly. Every man, woman, and child he came across were slaughtered. It was horrific, and necessary. King Eystein needed to know what he was dealing with, what sort of anger he had unleashed by killing the sons of Ragnar Lodbrok.

Invariably, though, some people escaped the onslaught and made it back to King Eystein.

And, along the way, Aslaug had begun to hear rumours about her husband. Worrying rumours that made her sleep unsettled as visions of him building a boat that would become his funeral pyre invaded her dreams.

CHAPTER 32:

EYSTEIN

"KING EYSTEIN!" THE WORDS WERE SHOUTED strongly across the marketplace. Eystein himself had heard his named called. He turned, and saw a bloody crumpled mess across from him. It seemed they had the strength to call out to him, but nothing more.

"Quick!" he instructed. "Help these men. Take them to the great hall and make sure they are tended to."

Eystein looked down at them while some of his attendants rushed forward to assist. Both men were young, they had probably been involved in a battle, he figured. He was not yet sure what danger was approaching, if any. They were his men, though; he knew this by their clothing. So, regardless of the real or perceived threat, they needed his attention.

Eystein walked back to the great hall, striding in front of the injured men. He seated himself and waited patiently. This is how he seemed to spend a lot of his time: waiting. So many people fought to become leaders or kings, thinking it were a noble and honourable life that was filled with fighting and excitement. Unfortunately, the reality was much more mundane.

The men were given water, fed a small meal and had their wounds looked at. Finally, King Eystein leaned forward.

"Tell me about your adventures," he queried.

One of the men stepped towards Eystein. "My name is

Reifnir and I am a member of your southern fleet. Yesterday, this fleet was attacked when men alighted from their own ships. They were fighting on behalf of Ragnar Lodbrok."

Eystein froze. He looked down on the man who had stepped back once more. "How do you know it is King Ragnar's troops?"

"The leader of this group was a boy who was hoisted up on a platform. His legs did not appear to be working."

It was Ivar the Boneless; he was sure of it. Eystein knew for certain then that Ragnar was seeking revenge for the death of his sons.

"We must ready for their imminent attack then. I thank you, Reifnir, for making the dangerous trek here to tell me this important news when you are so badly injured. Please, take advantage of my hospitality and make sure you are fully recovered before you leave. I will spare you nothing in the meantime"

Eystein suspected he was about to fight the biggest battle of his life. Moreover, it was because of a drunken betrothal. He shook his head at the stupidity of it all. He wondered if he should have just let Ragnar back out of marrying Ingibjorg. However, it would have been impossible to bargain with his daughter's honour. Truly, there was no way out of the coil, nor had there ever been. Some might have thought Ragnar had backed out because she was not worthy of him. Eystein tried to right the mess, to make some semblance of compromise by offering his same daughter to Eirik when they attacked. He wished Ragnar's son had seen reason and married Ingibjorg. However, that hadn't eventuated and, here they were about to go to war and end a lifelong friendship in the process.

There was no going back for Eystein. Just as there was no

question, they would fight until one of them was victorious, and the other was dead.

CHAPTER 33:

ℑVAR

IVAR LOOKED ON, READYING HIMSELF FOR battle. He could see Sibilja as she was brought forward. What happened next would decide the outcome of the battle entirely, so Ivar had no room for error. One tiny mistake could ruin everything.

He glanced over at his mother. Aslaug's face was white with fear. She had never seen this side of war and the last few weeks had opened her eyes to the atrocities of the battlefront. One night she had pleaded with him, asking that he spare the women and small children at least. Ivar had tried to explain that they had to appear strong. Any sign of weakness or even generosity would give Eystein the upper hand.

This led to an argument, and Aslaug left. In the morning, she had not relented, but neither had she blocked his way when they set off to loot another town. Perhaps she had come to understand it had to be done.

However, Ivar had no more time left for thoughts of his mother as Sibilja was released. She surged forward, bellowing as she did so. As soon as the cow opened her mouth, Ivar swung his sword. Everyone around him started beating their weapons against their shields. They roared out loudly as well, anything to help cover the sound of the howling beast.

"Now!" Ivar roared out his instruction. His platform bearers, three on each side of him, ran forward as fast as they could. They screamed the entire time in order to cover up the sound of Sibilja, who was approaching them at a rapid rate. Normally, Eystein would keep his cow close to him, the noise being enough to do the hard work for him. However, since Ivar had devised a way to cover up the sound of her, King Eystein had thrust the animal forward, whipping her rump and encouraging Sibilja to race forward, closer to the army in the hope her noise would overcome them.

This was exactly what Aslaug and Ivar had hoped for.

With Sibilja in reach, he asked his men to launch him forward, towards the animal. Two things could happen: either he would die, or he would land close enough to the beast that he could do some real damage.

Ivar felt the swoosh and tug as he ricocheted through the air. It felt like nothing he had ever experienced before. He yelled out—not in fright, but in sheer joy at the sensation. Perhaps this was what running felt like.

Landing close to the animal, Ivar grabbed his crossbow and loaded it up. He had to work quickly but, also, he had to work carefully. If he slipped while loaded the weapon, the cow would be on him and he would be trampled to death. Ivar roared as he worked, thrusting the bolt into the crossbow. He glanced quickly at Sibilja and saw she was coming closer still. Pulling up his weapon, he took aim. Ivar didn't have much time to line it up but he took a few more valuable seconds to make sure he only needed one shot. It was a fine line for Ivar as he crouched in the mud of battle and launched a bolt.

It launched through the air, flying so quickly that Ivar saw the cow fall before he could really follow the weapon's trajectory.

Sibilja hit the ground with a thud and silence enveloped

them. Silence from the animal and silence from Eystein's army. Not from Ivar's side, though. Instead, an almighty roar rose up from the throats of his men as they charged forward, victorious.

While the death of Sibilja was a great victory, Ivar's men still had to fight hard in order to defeat Eystein's army. For while the king relied on the cow to bring them victory, they were still well-trained in the way of fighting.

Ivar knew this and sent his men in with renewed vigour. He instructed them to scream as loud as they could and throw their weight around as though it was their very last effort ever before they entered Valhalla. He told them to behave as if they had already entered the hallowed halls, that their efforts would be renewed and they would fight as if they would never risk dying.

It was enough to rally the men, who turned into berserkers as they hit the battlefield. They pitched their weapons this way and that, causing so much calamity that it was hard to tell one body part from another as a sea of blood and human flesh engulfed the field.

Ivar heard many of the Swedes exclaim, as they died, that they had never fought such a battle in all their lives. Ragnar's son smiled whenever he heard this, pride swelling as he looked around the battle scene and took it all in.

They were winning, of that he was certain. So many of Eystein's men had fallen that their victory was imminent. When Ivar saw the few remaining troops start to turn and flee, he laughed so cruelly it sent chills down the spines of those on his own side.

Finally, Eystein was captured. Ivar's men brought him forward and Ivar, who was perched back on his platform, reached out with his crossbow. It was loaded and ready. He shot one bolt and it flew through the air, true to its cause. It struck Eystein in the chest and he dropped quickly, his body disappearing in the blood and gore at his feet.

His men cheered, great whoops of excitement that was accentuated by shouts and fists being swung in the air. Many of his men hugged each other outright.

Ivar looked around. A few of King Eystein's men stood around, as if unsure of what they should do: flee or die alongside their king.

"Your defeat has been a vicious one," Ivar shouted over the crowd. "However, I will not be so cruel as to make you suffer any more. I offer all of Eystein's army who still lives and stands among us, safe passage. I will not hunt you down and I will not hold you accountable for your ruler's actions. So, I offer you a truce."

While Ivar was sincere in his words, it appeared that many of Eystein's men did not believe him. They took no chances and all decided it was time to flee the scene. Ivar laughed as they left, laughing so hard he almost rolled off his platform.

"It's time for us to leave," he said once he'd stopped laughing. The thrill of victory mixed with the horror of the battleground to create a feeling in Ivar that left him thirsting for more "This land is now leaderless and I want to spend not a moment longer here. Let's find out if there are any greater forces that need attending to."

Ivar's men started packing up, looting the fallen and helping their own injured. Aslaug sidled up next to Ivar as they set foot for camp.

"You did well today, son," she said, a broad smile on her face. "Thank you for all your efforts. Now, as a result, we are finally free of Eystein."

"We are, dear mother. I am thankful you pushed me into

this battle. Ragnar's sons needed to be avenged and now it is likely we will get an even greater reputation." Ivar returned his mother's smile. "But, what of you now? You did well on the battlefield and directed everyone to a great victory. Perhaps you should continue on with us?"

Aslaug walked for a while, her feet silent as they stepped over rocks and grass alike. Ivar's men, on the other hand, were noisy and clumsy as they carried him over the same territory. It was moments like these that he resented the fact he couldn't walk.

"Son, it has been great fun and such an experience to join you in battle. However, I must head home now. Ragnar will surely be there, and wondering where we have all gone to."

While it was true, what Aslaug said, Ivar could see that she regretted her words. He suspected, if given the chance, if he pushed the matter hard enough, she would join him and his brothers as they continued in their efforts to uphold Ragnar's kingdom.

But, Ivar didn't push her. Instead, he reached out and held her hand as they travelled back to camp.

CHAPTER 34:

℞AGNAR

"WHERE IS MY WIFE?" RAGNAR ASKED AS SOON as he returned home. He was eager to discuss the meeting of kings with Aslaug.

"She's not here, Ragnar," Olaf answered. He was an old man now and hadn't travelled with Ragnar this time. "There were troubles with Sweden and she's had to deal with them. Please, step inside and I'll discuss it all with you."

It was bad news; Ragnar knew it as soon as Olaf wanted to talk about it away from the crowd.

"What's happened?" he demanded once they were through the doors of the great hall. He took a seat, waiting for the brunt of it.

"Firstly, I need to inform you that your son, Rognvald, is dead. He was welcomed in Valhalla after a raid in Hvitabaer."

Ragnar stopped breathing for a moment. The roaring in his ears drowned out the sound of everything else so it appeared to him like the whole world paused along with him.

"There is further bad news as well, I am afraid," Olaf continued. Ragnar leaned as far forward in his seat as was permissible, his breath now jagged with fear. "Agnar and Eirik went to defend yourself and your wife's good name against King Eystein. They fought a valiant fight, but, unfortunately, they were no match against King Eystein and his war cow, Sibilja. I am sorry to inform you that these sons also reside in the great halls of Valhalla."

Ragnar slumped back into his chair. He could feel the great wall of desolation as it crashed over him. His sons were gone. Thora's sons were gone, which was harder to fathom. The very last part of Thora left in this world was now obsolete, taken from him because of a stupid drunken proposal—and not even one of his own. He wanted to kill Rolf and he would the next time he saw him, Ragnar decided. But, Olaf was talking again and Ragnar had to focus on his words, knowing there was more to come.

"When the remains of Eirik and Agnar's army returned, Aslaug and her boys set off for Sweden with a plan to finish King Eystein once and for all."

Ragnar couldn't breathe at this point. He knew all about Sibilja, had witnessed her horrible bellowing firsthand the last time he visited with Eystein. The sound was unbearable and made him want to do horrible things. Ragnar gnashed his teeth and waited to be told the rest of his family was dead as well. His whole body felt numb and he couldn't hear the words that Olaf spoke. It was as if he stood at the end of a field and Olaf was all the way across the other side, the distance not only a hindrance, as the wind whipped away his words. Sighing heavily, Ragnar pulled himself forward once more.

"Your son, Ivar, was successful. He managed to not only defeat Sibilja, but also kill King Eystein. Your wife and her children all survived the onslaught."

"Pardon?" Ragnar was sure he was imagining things. How could they survive Eystein's army with Sibilja at the head of it? He shook his head, wondering if he was going mad with grief.

"Aslaug, Ivar, and the rest of your sons survived the

attack. Sibilja is dead, along with the king of Sweden."

Ragnar felt the world start to move again. So, it was true. His family lived on, or most of them anyway. He still couldn't think too much about Rognvald, Agnar, and Eirik. Grieving for them would come later, he knew. Ragnar listened while Olaf regaled him with the heroics of his sons as they overcame King Eystein. It was a welcome distraction, something to concentrate his energies on so he wasn't drawn into thinking about all he had just lost.

The grief subsided as he listened and something else started to grow in its place: resentment. Here Ragnar was, one of the greatest kings of their time, and yet, his sons were already beginning to surpass him. He may have raided hard and conquered many lands. He may have also defeated the great lindworm surrounding Thora's bower and gained the moniker, Lodbrok. However, here was Ivar, leading his brothers at an earlier age than Ragnar had been when he started his leadership and defeating the magical Sibilja—at an earlier age than he had defeated Thora's lindworm.

Ragnar sat back, welcoming the jealousy over the anguish of losing three of his sons. Here was something he could concentrate on, something more than his grief. This jealousy was probably of his own making in order to smother the heartache he was not ready to be engulfed by. He didn't want to think about the loss of his first sons, the ones to Thora, because it felt like losing his first wife all over again.

"Olaf!" Ragnar interrupted the man while he spoke. He had heard enough of his sons amazing deeds and was now ready to create some of his own. "I have a plan."

The plan was rash and impetuous. It was probably dangerous and stupid also. However, Ragnar felt overcome by the need to do something, much in the same way he had done so when Thora first died. He knew he could channel his tremulous pain and do great things with it. This time, though, he didn't want to raid like he normally did. He had done enough of that already and so had many of those around him. Every skald that visited talked of raiding and the successes that came from the danger of it. No, he wanted to do something entirely different. He wanted to do something so dangerous and amazing that people would never stop talking about the famous Ragnar Lodbrok ever again.

He was going to sail to England. Ragnar Lodbrok was going to invade and conquer England.

Moreover, he would accomplish this by using only two ships.

CHAPTER 35:

ᚼSLAUG

"HUSBAND, I AM HOME!" ASLAUG BREEZED into the great hall. "I have travelled a great distance and done many wonderful things. However, on my return voyage here, I have heard some interesting whispers about you and the two ships you are building. What is going on?"

Once she laid eyes on him, though, her grief overtook everything. She rushed forward and as she approached, Aslaug saw the tears there and knew that Ragnar was suffering at the loss of his children. She allowed her own tears to fall as anguish coursed through her body. They embraced fiercely with their combined distress.

"We killed him, Ragnar. We killed King Eystein. Your sons have been avenged."

"I know." Ragnar whispered the words softly into her ear. She could feel the wet of his tears in her hair and reached up to wipe his face. Her hand lingered as she stared into his eyes. Her tears subsided as she allowed herself to be lost in them for a moment.

Ragnar hadn't changed a bit since she saw him last, but she checked twice anyway, more so she could drink in his handsome features and remind herself once more how lucky she was. But, all she saw when she looked him over was Eirik. Eirik, who would never be Ragnar's age now. Her lips trembled.

The last time they had embraced, three of Ragnar's sons had still been alive. Aslaug felt a sob tearing up her throat once more. She fell on him, burying herself in his shoulder, trying to hide her emotion from him. His scent, the unmistakable aroma that was Ragnar, helped to squash down her grief. Ragnar knew though, she could tell in the way he pulled her in tighter, his fingers tangling in her long hair and brushing the nape of her neck. This was how he always comforted her.

"What whispers have you heard, dear wife?" Ragnar finally asked as he pulled free from her. Aslaug felt relief at the fact Ragnar had drawn them away from the loss of their children. She was not ready to talk about them yet, not with the one person who would feel their loss as fiercely as her own. Aslaug swallowed down the lump in her throat.

"The surrounding lands are concerned at the size of the ships you are building. There is talk you plan to invade them." Ragnar laughed at her words. Aslaug reached out and touched his arm, still not quite done with the novelty of him after all this time. She stroked his hand and then laced her fingers through his.

"You have heard half-truths. I have no plans to raid my neighbours," Ragnar said when he was finished laughing. "Plus, there are only two of them, not a fleet at all."

"Then why are you building such large boats?" The creeping terror of her hazy premonition washed over her. Aslaug could not understand why ships of that size would be built unless it was to intimidate the surrounding kingdoms. Especially considering there was only a couple of them.

"I plan to invade England." Ragnar turned and looked at her. Aslaug tried to determine if any early signs of madness were present in his face, or if it was just in his words.

"With two ships? What sort of nonsense is this? You can't invade England without a full fleet." A chill was starting to settle in her bones.

"Since I have been away, my sons and you have been busy making legends for the skalds to talk about. Well, I have decided that it is my turn to create amazing stories. I will take my two ships and conquer England. Imagine if I manage to achieve my goal. There is no glory for those who raid and conquer using a full-sized fleet."

"This seems like a very foolish plan, Ragnar." Aslaug was nervous. She pulled her hand free of Ragnar's and started to chew on her fingers. "There is no need for more glory, you are already celebrated among our people for all the heroic deeds you have performed and all the lands you have defeated."

"Yes, I may have done many great things, but people are tired of those stories. It is time to attempt something even more astounding than I have already achieved."

"I think you need to reconsider your plans. I do not feel good at all about this journey. You know how troublesome it is to travel to England in our ships. Even with a full fleet, you will lose many to the treachery of the shores there. Moreover, if you wreck your ships, and still manage to survive the journey, I am sure the English kings there will see fit to arrest you immediately. Especially that King Aelle, after you killed his father all those years ago. Do you really want that?"

"Let the gods decide my fate, dear Aslaug. I am ready for this journey and I need it." Aslaug could see the grief in his face as he spoke these words and wondered if he would still be so foolish as to come up with this idea if his sons had not just died. "Plus, if I do not succeed at my task, it will have only been two ships and the men I can fit into them that will be lost."

That is what Aslaug feared the most. Even as Ragnar spoke the words, she could feel the trueness of them rising up from her frigid bones and coiling around her neck. She couldn't breathe for the knowing that this journey would be like no other that Ragnar had attempted. And, not for the reason he thought. There would be no glory for Ragnar in this trip, although, he would be right about the story-telling afterwards. Oh, how people would talk about this trip. But, not for the glory of it.

For Aslaug could only see the black raven of death flying high over Ragnar's head.

CHAPTER 36:

$\mathfrak{A}$SLAUG

ASLAUG HAD DREADED THE DAY WHEN Ragnar would leave their home in search of infamy in England. Yet, here she was, the day before and still furiously stitching a vest for him.

She spent many days searching for all the things needed for this special piece of clothing. At the marketplace, Aslaug had begged traders to search out items for her. She paid much more than the materials were worth for the haste of their delivery.

The shirt would be Ragnar's lifeline, Aslaug hoped. She had poured her heart into it and hoped it would be enough to save his life. Yet, she told no one for this item needed to be created in the world but outside of it. If another living person happened upon what she was doing, she would have to cast it aside and begin again for fear the enchantment she worked into it wouldn't be fulfilled.

Ever since Ragnar had concocted this idea to conquer England, Aslaug felt a dread in the pit of her stomach. It sat there as if she had swallowed a stone. Only this stone was a living thing and it grew each day as she saw improvement on the duo of ships Ragnar planned to take with him.

"I wish you would hold off on your travel, Ragnar." Aslaug tried one last time to get Ragnar to stay behind and give up on this fateful journey.

"You know I cannot do that, Aslaug," Ragnar replied as he started to undress. It was late and Aslaug wanted to stay awake all night, for this night to never end, for light never to be borne on the land again so that it would not be tomorrow and Ragnar wouldn't leave her again.

"Then, the least you can do is love me tonight." She stifled the tears that seemed ever-present lately.

Aslaug reached up and started to unlace her clothing as Ragnar strode over to her. She reached out for him, her robes falling away from her and revealing her bare flesh.

"I will miss you, Aslaug." His voice was husky, and it was all Aslaug could do to stop the dam of tears from overflowing. She leaned in to kiss him, distracting herself in an effort to delay her anguish. Their lips crashed together like the treacherous waves of the English shoreline.

Their bodies mingled, a familiar and welcome blend as their kisses intensified. Aslaug let her fingers roam over Ragnar's body, exploring and rediscovering him. Ragnar did the same, searching out those places he loved to caress. One hand traced up her arm and then down over her clavicles until it reached that section of her torso where the hardness of her ribs gave way to the softness of her breasts. She shivered in delicious anticipation.

Aslaug sighed as the tingle of excitement grew within her. And, for the first time in many weeks, she lost herself up completely to the sensation of her body, and his, rather than the sadness of knowing she would be losing him soon.

She kissed him deeply, her tongue probing as her hands ran over the hardness of his shoulders and down his back to where she could feel the roundness of his behind, still as rock hard as the rest of him. Aslaug felt the tears forming again. It would be such a waste, this fine body, to be lost so soon.

She was selfish and didn't want Ragnar to find fame in Valhalla. All she wanted was to grow old with this man, the one who had saved her from her childhood and brought her back into the world of the living. Tears escaped in earnest then, but it didn't matter anymore because Ragnar had laid her down on their bed and was entering her.

Nothing mattered beyond this moment and her tears were lost in their passion.

"I HAVE A GIFT for you, husband."

It was morning. The dreaded light had returned in spite of all her begging. It seemed that the gods were not about to grant her the one thing she wanted more than anything else in this world.

"What is it, Aslaug?" Ragnar's fingers were gently caressing her shoulder. They were still lying in bed and she was trying her best to delay the inevitable. Aslaug rolled over and kissed him on the nose before getting out of bed. She was still naked from their night of lovemaking and she hoped it would coerce Ragnar into staying a little longer. When he did not reach for her, Aslaug strode across the room.

"It is a shirt I have been making for you ever since you announced you would head off on this crazy journey of yours." Aslaug pulled the item free from one of the baskets at the end of the bed.

"I have no need of a new shirt. I have plenty of them already." Ragnar sat up in bed and the furs fell away from his body. Aslaug stood there, shirt in one hand and stared at him.

"Ragnar, I will miss you terribly while you are gone. I will count down the days until we shall meet again. But, I ask of you that you wear this shirt for the entirety of your journey. You know I have misgivings about this trip and I fear I will never see you again, especially if you remove the shirt I have made for you. I have stitched it with magic and had it blessed by the gods." Aslaug paused, her voice choking and betraying her emotion. "It is only a small thing I ask of you."

Ragnar stood up. Striding over, he wrapped his arms around her. "I will miss you greatly too, dear wife. I always do when I am parted from you. But, have no fear, I will be back home before you know it and filled to the brim with amazing tales to tell."

"Perhaps you will, or perhaps the gods will steal you away from me. However, I beg of you, please wear this shirt. I have spent such a great amount of time on it. So, if nothing more, grant me this wish so I have not wasted all of my efforts on it. I have threaded the shirt with hoar-grey strands of hair, and as long as you shall wear it, no wound you receive will be bloody, nor will any weapons bite you."

He looked down, his eyes bearing into hers. She stared back at him earnestly. Getting Ragnar to wear this shirt was the singular most important thing in her entire life. "I can see how much this means to you, Aslaug. Don't worry, I will wear your shirt, and wear it with pride."

Later that day, when Ragnar boarded his ship and waved goodbye, Aslaug held tight to her sons and cried. Her sobs could be heard across the dock and all the way out to sea. She did not hold back, this one last time she would lay eyes on her husband.

Ragnar stared back at her, anguish on his face. Yet he remained on the ship and allowed it to take him out to sea and away from her.

CHAPTER 37:

ℜAGNAR

THE KNARRS HAD TRAVELLED WELL OVER the water and Ragnar was proud of his boats. However, workmanship is often not enough when it came to the treacherous perils of the gods. A terrible storm erupted as they were nearing England. It rose up, a sheer physical force of brutal winds and frigid rain. Ragnar and his men fought hard against the onslaught. Their bodies were soaked through and the winds whipped their clothes around, slapping, and snapping against skin reddened from the harsh rain.

It felt like a whole day had passed as Ragnar battled the elements, trying to save his ships and the men aboard them. He knew it was a losing battle though. The destructive force of the weather was all around him; punishing him until he was convinced the storm was an actual god, angry with him over something for which he had no idea.

His ships wheezed and cracked around him. The battle to control them as well as avoid falling debris and flying shrapnel was now an added struggle. Ragnar yelled at his men, at the storm itself, and tried to keep them all alive.

"I can see the shore!" Ragnar had been shooting surreptitious glances whenever he could in the hope they were closer to land than he envisioned. He had caught a few furtive shadows he thought were cliffs before he finally laid eyes on the dark sands of England.

"Where are we?" someone shouted.

Ragnar had no idea. He could see churned up beach and cliffs to either side. Scanning the water, he suddenly felt cold.

"Rocks, directly ahead!"

There was no need to explain further. All of his crew stopped what they were doing and grabbed at whatever they could. Ragnar and another man hugged the mast. Others grabbed the sides of the longship, their knuckles white as they clung to the vessel, desperately trying to stay alive.

The impact shot through Ragnar's bones with the force of every rock they hit. He felt like his tightly clenched teeth were chipping away with each blow beneath his feet.

As soon as they struck English sand, Ragnar jumped from the dilapidated ship. He dropped to the ground, his body heaving with his exhaustion. There was no need to secure what was left of the Knarrs, so battered they were from the storm. He slumped there for a long time, his crew scattered around him. All of them were resting in an effort to recover from the storm. As his breath relaxed and became less laboured, Ragnar started to smile.

He was alive and others were too.

"I can smell adventure, can't you?" Ragnar finally said. He rolled over onto his back and watched the roiling clouds above him, inhaling deeply of the salty air.

"It always smells like adventure once you jump from a seafaring ship," Leif replied. "But, really, it is just the relief at no longer having to smell piss and old sweat."

Ragnar laughed. "I suspect you are right." But, he could feel it; excitement uncoiling from his toes and up through his body, the sensation that something big was headed his way. They had survived against all odds. It was proof this journey was fated and that his life was important. His fingers tingled in anticipation.

"Up you get!" His fingers continued to tingle, but this time it was because a sword was held to his throat.

ᛗ

THE STORM HAD FINALLY eased as Ragnar stared up at the man attached to the sword. It was still dismal weather, however, as it was always that way in England. The colour that reminded Ragnar most of England was grey. This shade was everywhere: in the clouds, in the fog encircling them, and in the smoke of fires that were constantly damp.

Ragnar glanced around him. Only a few other men accompanied this one. They all carried highly crafted weapons and their clothes were well made. These men likely belonged to an earl or English king, he decided. But, they were only a small group. Out of the corner of his eye, he could see movement from his crew. They were coiled, ready to spring, even if they did not look it.

"Are you here to welcome me to your fine land?" Ragnar asked.

"Our king wants—" Ragnar rolled out from under the sword. His men also sprang to life, each man rolling before jumping up and grabbing the small group before they had gotten over the surprise.

"I really don't care what your king wants," Ragnar replied. He pulled a knife free from his waist, thanking the gods it had not been lost to the storm. He plunged it deeply to its hilt and watched as the colour drained from the man's face.

"It seems the English know we are here already. Our good manners have preceded us." Ragnar winked at his men. "We must make haste then."

They ran from the shore, anticipating a larger group of men to be ready to ambush them but there were none. It must have been a small scouting group, Ragnar decided. "They knew we were coming, but not that we would be here so soon, it seems."

While they would have liked to stop and loot the bodies, Ragnar decided against it. They needed to find a town. Somewhere bigger that would have the supplies they now needed.

Ragnar's body was weary even though exhilaration coursed through him. This was the very sort of adventure he had been anticipating. He smiled as he ran, and thought of Aslaug—as he had last seen her, distraught on the shore. Instead, he remembered their lovemaking from the night before he sailed, the way she had arched underneath him and smiled as they drifted off to sleep. Ragnar grinned at her now as he looked skyward and promised her he would return. He pushed the thought out through the air, hoping it would catch a breeze and she would hear him. If there was anyone who could listen to him this way, it was his dear wife.

The first town they reached was too small even to warrant the title. It was good enough though.

Ragnar and his men had sneaked up as the light was fading from the sky and slit the throats of whoever crossed their paths. It didn't take long to secure the place. They feasted there and recuperated overnight. The next morning, when their bellies were full and their muscles replenished from a good night's sleep, they plotted their next moves.

During the next few weeks, Ragnar and his men terrorised their location. They slaughtered those in each town they came to and laughed at those that managed to escape. Let them spread their stories, Ragnar had reminded his small army. After all, it was notoriety Ragnar was after. There was no point making it to England in only two Knarrs if he planned to lay low. He wanted to conquer this place and incite fear into the locals.

Over time, Ragnar heard whispers from those they tortured before killing. King Aelle was the king that first man had been talking about when they were captured on the shores of England. This gave Ragnar pause. So, it was personal then, he decided. Ragnar had killed Aelle's father many years ago and it was likely he was seeking retribution for the death.

Further news revealed that Aelle knew Ragnar had left Norway thanks to the story spreading about his preposterous idea of conquering England with such a small army. Therefore, King Aelle was anticipating an attack and that's why they had encountered the small group on their arrival. Now time was of the essence. Ragnar needed to gather his troops and fight smartly against people that knew the land better than he did.

He assigned men to skirt the town they had most recently looted. They needed to know when another larger group was approaching. Ragnar knew it was only a matter of time before his men would clash with Aelle's and he relished the thought.

"We must prepare for battle," Ragnar said, but he wasn't worried. They had killed enough men now be able to dress themselves in armour. When they looted, they found more weapons than they could carry. In fact, they had even returned to the wrecks of the longships and managed to reclaim some of their equipment. Ragnar looked across at his old spear. It was the one he had used, all those long years ago, to slay Thora's lindworm. More good fortune, he figured as he thanked the gods for its safety. He smiled at the memory of Thora before drawing himself back to the group.

Their only weakness was their numbers. Ragnar looked around at the group as he rubbed the edge of his shirt, the one Aslaug had made. He felt safe within it, as he looked around at the strong men all ready to fight. However, Ragnar knew the odds. It was likely many men would perish once Aelle's army attacked. But, he also knew it was their way. It was the only way to score victory in Valhalla.

A messenger approached.

"What is it, Gnup?"

The man sat down before speaking. "Aelle's forces are approaching."

Ragnar smiled as his fingers rubbed the course fabric of his shirt once more. So far, it had held true to Aslaug's magic, no weapon had come close to causing him injury on this journey. He was confident his luck would continue. He grabbed the spear he had used to slay Thora's serpent and leapt up to meet his fate.

CHAPTER 38:

ᚨELLE

"ON THIS DAY, I WANT RAGNAR SPARED!" KING Aelle roared it out over his army. "Make no mistake about this man; he has many sons who would wreak havoc on England if we were to slaughter him. Kill his men, but leave him alive."

Aelle frowned as his men stood around him. He needed to make a stand against the dreaded Northmen, to demonstrate how strong England was against them. After all, they had been a scourge on their lands for as long as he could remember. He blanched a little then, remembering his first encounter with the abhorrent pagans. It had been a battle like no other he had ever seen in his young life, the one in which the cursed Ragnar had killed his father, Hame. For that, he could never forgive the man.

He had to work out what he would do with Ragnar once he caught him. Aelle knew Ragnar had many sons. Those sons were strong and feared across lands more diverse than just England. Killing him outright in retaliation for his father's death was not a viable option, unfortunately. While Ragnar himself was an impressive man, with stories of his varied feats well known in England, a group headed by his sons was likely more than his army could handle all at once. And, this is what would happen if Aelle were to kill him.

Aelle stood taller, his eyes casting a searching glance over his men. His group was big, but probably not large enough against Ragnar's sons. No, he had to make sure Ragnar lived.

Now was not the time to make a decision, though. Instead, he led his men out to the battleground. He smiled as he saw the paltry number of men in Ragnar's army.

"Our victory is already assured!" he roared as the battle commenced.

Aelle looked everywhere for Ragnar. Each man blended into the next and none stood out via their clothing to indicate a higher stature.

While Aelle had never laid eyes on Ragnar, he had heard many stories about him. Not only were his fighting skills impressive, he was supposed to be incredibly handsome. Aelle imagined he was very lucky with female companionship, although he really didn't know to whom he was married to right now, or, if he even had a wife. However, he had heard stories about the many feats he had gone through to win women, so it seemed likely there was another wife already, after the death of the one who had the snakes.

Returning his sight to the battlefield, Aelle observed his men, who seemed confused also. While they had been given an order, they also seemed unable to identify the Norse leader. In the end, his men simply fought the invaders. As a result, Aelle anticipated he would have to battle Ragnar's sons at some point in time. He gulped in nervous anticipation.

Regardless of Aelle's concerns, it was an easy battle. His men, once committed, though, had slashed the small group down until they were nothing more than a bloody pile. By the end of it, only one man remained standing.

Aelle approached, intrigued. The man appeared to be wearing nothing more than a ragged old shirt and a pair of blood-smeared pants.

"Who are you?" Aelle demanded. The man remained silent as he smirked at him. The king felt his annoyance rising.

"I demand to know who you are!" His words roared out more harshly than he anticipated; his irritation already on display. The man laughed in reply.

"I am no one of concern to you, King Aelle."

Aelle stared at the man. His hands clenched together into fists at his sides as he did so.

"If you will not tell me who you are, then I will put you through a great trial. It will be one so horrific that you will give up your name in the end." Aelle had his suspicions about who stood before him and had devised a plan on the spot using inspiration from one of the stories about Ragnar himself. "I will cast you forth into a pit of snakes. There you shall sit. While no weapon seemed to bite you today, the snakes in the pit most surely will."

"BUT WHAT IF IT really is the leader?" One of Aelle's men asked him.

"We will keep a close eye on him. If he says anything that could indicate he is Ragnar, we will pull him free." Aelle was sure the man in the ragged shirt was indeed Ragnar Lodbrok. He leaned forward and glared down at the man in the bottom of the pit. "Release the snakes!"

With large bags in their hands, several men leaned over the deep hole. Unknotting the necks, they released the serpents into the pit.

Stepping up to the edge once the snakes were all safely in the pit, Aelle observed the man. He smiled still. The snakes twined around him, wriggling and slithering over each other as they moved away from him. Aelle's brow knotted together. Perhaps they weren't really moving away from him. Maybe it just seemed that way.

He beckoned to the man beside him. "Poke those snakes and make sure they are up close to him."

The man did as he was told. However, each time the snakes were pushed towards the man in the pit, they immediately slithered away when the stick was pulled back. It was blatantly obvious the snakes were avoiding him.

Aelle didn't know what to do. He gazed at the figure below, who still smiled up at him. He was tall and built like a man who had fought hard all of his life. Scars lined his face and down his neck, where they disappeared under the collar of his shirt. Aelle paused.

"There is unholy magic upon this man. Remove his shirt!"

The cocky smile faltered with Aelle's words. It was now the king's turn to be happy. The man was hoisted from the pit and his shirt cut from him.

When he was thrown back into the hole, the snakes hissed and headed straight for him. A frenzy of scales and tails and sharp teeth descended on the Northman.

Aelle leaned in close, ready to grab the man out if he should give up his identity.

As he did so, the man started to talk.

CHAPTER 39:

Ragnar

RAGNAR FELT THE STING OF FANGS AS THE snakes descended on him. He bit the inside of his mouth, determined not to show weakness in front of King Aelle. Instead, he thought of Aslaug and how she had begged him not to come here, not to let his foolish pride and ambition cloud his judgement. He smiled bitterly as he remembered her words. Ragnar wished he could have died while still wearing her shirt, so that it would feel like she was covering him and holding him as he was drawn into Valhalla.

Grimly, Ragnar started to speak. He looked up at Aelle, maintaining eye contact with him. Each line pushed out with ragged breaths.

> "Tackled my enemies in,
> More than fifty battles, I have,
> A splendid feat, so many did call,
> As I have killed many great men,
> Yet, a simple snake, here in a pit,
> Will end me now,
> Life is strange, though,
> And things are most unexpected."

His words were just fancy nothings, other than the line about how many battles he had fought. Aelle had his answer now about his true identity. Yet, Ragnar continued to speak.

"If the piglets knew the punishment of the boar, surely they would break into the sty to free him," he wheezed as the snakes continued to attack him. Even though the blistering agony of multiple searing bites, Ragnar could see the recognition bleed into Aelle's face. He knew the English king was fearful of the wrath of his sons for he had overheard him talking earlier.

"Pull him up! Pull him up!" Frantically, two men started to haul Ragnar out of the pit. It was too late though as the adders had found ghastly substance in the fibres of his entrails. Still, Ragnar continued to taunt the king.

> "Now cease our song—the Goddesses come,
> And invite me home to the Hall of Odin;
> Happy there, on a high-raised throne,
> Seated with gods, I shall quaff my ale,
> The hours of my life have passed away,
> And in joyous laughter shall I die."[1]

And then, Ragnar died. His body slumped forward, the weight causing the men to drop the ropes supporting him and he toppled back into the snake pit.

The screech of a raven above sounded like the scream of a woman.

---

[1] O'Clery, M., CONNELLAN, O., MACDERMOTT, P. and O'MULCONRY, F. (1846). *The Annals of Ireland [from A.D. 1171 to A.D. 1616]. Translated from the original Irish of the Four Masters by O'Connellan, with annotations by P. MacDermott and the translator.* Dublin, p.462.

EPILOGUE

"NO!" ASLAUG SCREAMED IT OUT, HER VOICE as ragged as a crow's caw. She dropped to the ground, her basket toppling, forgotten, from her hands. Its contents scattered around her, creating a treacherous barrier.

"Mother, what is it?" Sigurd called out to her as he cleared a path through the debris.

"Your father is dead." Aslaug wailed some more, her throat already raw from the emotional release.

She felt her youngest son's arms envelop her and she leaned into his shoulder, her grief overwhelming. Sigurd did not question her, there was no need as her grief was evidence enough that her words were honest. And so they sat there, with Aslaug sobbing inconsolably for the longest time.

People started to gather. They saw her desolation and patted her back. All joined together as their world began to mourn the loss of one of their own kind, one that would soon pass into legend for lifetimes to come.

For Ragnar had a long-lasting legacy. Even as Aslaug wept, she knew this to be true. She may have considered Ragnar her greatest love, but the world could now claim him. Along with Ragnar's legacy, his boys were already warriors and stepping out to make their mark on the world—known and unknown.

Regardless, Aslaug sobbed.

PART TWO

THE HISTORICAL FACTS

WHO WERE THE VIKINGS?

When one thinks of the Vikings, quite often the first thing they think of is how violent they were. Known as barbarians who raped, pillaged and looted wherever they set foot, popular culture has done little to explore beyond these stereotypes. Considering some of what is known about the Vikings has been written and handed down via Christian sources, it could be possible that the Vikings were merely the brunt of religious propaganda rather than the bloodthirsty descriptive we have come to associate with them.

Also, it is possible the Vikings were a group of people that had very good reasons for doing what they did. Regardless of why the Vikings were so violent, it is known they invaded various parts of Europe before branching out and raiding as far away as the Mediterranean, North Africa, the Middle East and Central Asia.

The Vikings were not actually a particular race but more a group of people that travelled from Scandinavia. This group was more defined by the fact they were considered foreign to England and the other countries they raided. Another component to grouping these raiders under the umbrella of "Viking" was the fact they weren't Christian.

The word "Viking," is generally considered by historians to come from the Scandinavian term "vikingr." To translate this term into English gives it the meaning of "pirate," or, alternatively, to mean those who are sea faring, or are a sea warrior, especially considering the word can be broken down further still into the Old Norse, "vik," meaning bay or creek. Therefore, it is possible this term has been translated in a way that has helped to perpetuate the villainy associated with the Vikings.

The term also represents a small percentage of the Norse population that later came to be known as "Vikings." For the sake of convenience in this section, I will be referring to the Norse populations of what became to be known as the Viking Age as "Vikings." In the second, fictional section, I will not be using the term "Viking" or "Vikings," however, as this is not how the people of that time referred to themselves. Instead, they will be referred to by their location as an identifier when required.

Originating in the Nordic section of Europe that includes Denmark, Finland, Iceland, Norway and Sweden, they raided across Europe between the late 8th century through to the late 11th century AD. In fact, the very first recorded Viking raid can be pinpointed to an attack on the abbey at Lindisfarne on 8 June 793. According to historical documents of the time, a scholar working in Frankia wrote a letter describing the attack to the king of Northumbria and the bishop of Lindisfarne.[2]

> "Pagans have desecrated God's sanctuary, shed the blood of saints around the altar, laid waste the house of our hope and trampled the bodies of saints like dung in the streets."

---

[2] S Allott (ed and trans), Alcuin of York: His Life and Letters (York, 1974), letter no. 26, 36–8, and also D Whitelock (ed and trans), English Historical Documents, vol 1: c 550–1042 (London, 1979), document no. 194, 778–9

During the time of the Viking Era, however, Denmark, Finland, Norway and Sweden were vastly different to the present day countries. Not only were some of these countries known by different names, but the boundaries were not set as rigidly as they are today. Being a time when the Christians were converting and there was constant disagreement within the Viking settlements over who ruled what areas, there was a certain fluidity to the borders. Added to this was the fact Vikings were known to fight among themselves over land parcels and rulership issues.

It is likely the Vikings began raiding for several reasons including the need for richer agricultural resources as well as retaliation against the Christian invasion that was attempting to extinguish their pagan beliefs. The introduction of the Viking Age to the rest of Europe occurred during what is known as the Medieval Warm Period. It also coincided with the advent of Charlemagne's Saxon Wars, an event that saw Christianity enforced throughout Europe. Therefore, the Vikings were, potentially, retaliating against a culture that was foreign to them as the Christians advanced on the pagans during this time.

Regardless of why the Vikings invaded Europe, the fact is they arrived there and managed to integrate into many positions of power; the perfect example of this is Duke Rollo. Rollo was later baptized as Robert and became the first king of Normandy, a region in France. Over time, the Vikings managed to adapt and assimilate themselves into various countries and cultures, disappearing from their initial identity as "sea-faring warriors." So, while the Viking era may have a fairly set end time, the Vikings were still there, adding their own special flavours to the cultures they had joined.

For the sake of the argument, though, it is considered the

Viking Age ended in England with the Norman conquest in 1066 at the Battle of Stamford Bridge. In Ireland, the era ended in 1171 with the capture of Dublin by Strongbow. 1263 saw the defeat of King Hákon Hákonarson at the Battle of Largs in Scotland which ended the era of the Vikings there. The Western Isles and the Isle of Man remained under Viking rule until 1266. Finally, Orkney and Shetland finally overthrew the king of Norway around 1469.

𝕬 MAP OF ASLAUG AND RAGNAR'S WORLD

The world that Aslaug and Ragnar lived in can been seen in the map below, using the common names for each area in the Viking Age as well as the places we now know them. Names in all capital letters, (i.e. SWEDEN) are the current titles. However, during the Viking Age, these areas were less defined or only known by the other name places indicated (i.e. Gotaland).

This map was originally developed from a public domain satellite image that was kindly provided by Koyos (commons.wikimedia.org/wiki/File:Norden_satellite.jpg).

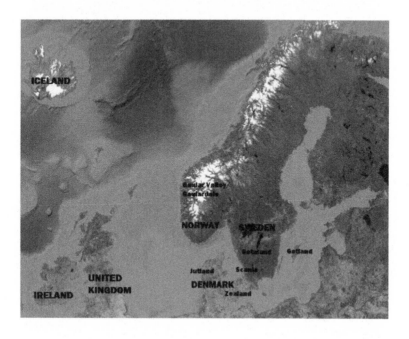

Some of the common alternative names for these areas can also be found below:

Gaular: Gaulardale, Gaular Valley, Fosselandet (the land of the waterfalls).
Götaland: Gotaland, Gautland, Gothia, Gothenland, Gothland.
Gotland: Gottland.
Skania: Skane, Skåne.
Jutland: Jütland, Cimbric or Cimbrian Peninsula, Den Kimbriske Halvø, Kimbrische Halbinsel, Cimbricus Chersonesus, Denmark.
Zealand: Sjælland, Denmark. It should be noted that Zealand should not be confused with Zeeland, which is located in Holland.

ALTERNATIVE NAMES

Those names marked with an asterisk (*) indicate this name could be associated with the person, but there is not a definitive distinction linking the person to the name.

Aslaug: Aslög, Aslog, Kráka, Kraka, Kraba, Randalin

Bjorn (Ragnar's son): Björn, Biorn, Bjorn Ironsides, Bjorn Ironside, Björn Ironside/s, Bjǫrn Járnsíða, Björn Járnsíða, Björn Järnsida, Bjørn Jernside; Bier Costae ferreae

Brynhildr: Brünhild, Brunnhilde, Brynhild, Brunhilda of Austrasia*, Sigrdrífa

Eirik (Ragnar's son): Eiríkr, Eric, Erik, Eirek Ragnarsson, interchangeable with Radbard and Dunwat

Eystein: King Eystein, Eysteinn, Eysteinn Beli, Eysteinn hinn illráði, Östen Illråde, Östen Beli

Hvitserk (Ragnar's son): Halfdan*

Herrud: King Herodd: King Herraud, King Herrauðr, Herrud, Herothus Heroth, Gautric

Ingibjorg: Ingeborg, Borghild

Ivar (Ragnar's son): Iwar, Ívarr hinn Beinlausi, Hyngwar, Ivar the Boneless, Ivar the Despicable, Ivar the Hated*, Ingvar*, Ímar*, Imar*

King Aelle: Ælla, Ælle, Alla, Aella

King Herodd: King Herraud, King Herrauðr, Herrud, Herothus Heroth, Gautric

Ragnar: Ragnar Lodbrok, Ragnar Lothbrok, Ragnar Loðbrók Ragnar Sigurdsson, Ragnar "Lodbrok"

Sigurdsson, Ragnarr Loðbrók, Ragnar Shaggy-Breeches, Regnerus, King Horik I*, King Reginfrid*, Reginherus*, Reginheri*, Rognvald*, Ragnall*, Lodebrochus*, Lothbrocus*

Sigurd: Sigurðr, Siward, Siggurd, Siegfried, Sivard Snarensven, Sivard Snarensvend, Sigfroðr, Sivard

Thora: Þóra Borgarhjǫrtr, Thora Borgarhjört, Thora Town-Hart, Fortress-Thora

Sigurd (Aslaug's Father): Siward, Siggurd, Sigurðr, Siegfried, Sivard Snarensven, Sigurd the Dragon Slayer

Sigurd (Ragnar's grandfather): Siward, Siggurd,

Sigurd Ring (Ragnar's Father): Siward Ring, Siggurd Ring, Sigurd Hring, Siggurd Hring,

Sigurd (Ragnar's son): Siward, Siggurd, Sigurd Snake-in-the-Eye

Thora: Þóra Borgarhjǫrtr, Thora Borgarhjört, Thora Town-Hart

Ubbe (Ragnar's son): Ubbi, Hubba, Ubba, Usto*

It also needs to be noted here that Ragnar potentially had two other sons: Halfdan (Halfdan Ragnarsson) and Rognald that cannot be firmly attributed to any of the sons mentioned above.

Additionally, Bjorn Ironside is a different figure to Bjørn Haraldsen Ironside.

HISTORICAL SOURCES

When approaching the sources in regard to the Vikings, historians have to battle many obstacles.

There are various historical sources of information from many different places. Some are English, others from the areas from which the Vikings originated. Each of these sources was written hundreds of years ago, and, therefore, have to be translated and interpreted not only because of the language, but also because of the cultural differences at the time.

Besides the obvious complications that arise form translating older versions of languages, there can be many varied interpretation errors. For example, simple things like phrasing can be translated in different ways.

Another complication with translating from old sources, is matching up various names. Names can vary between manuscripts and this can be dependent on many different reasons. The Viking sagas have been written down after the events, sometimes by many hundreds of years. Quite often, these events occurred in different countries or were transcribed by people in different locations, meaning names can be changed depending on the language used. A perfect example of this is Aslaug's father, Sigurd. Some of his stories have been written down in German and the name Siegfried is used in place of the more common Sigurd or Siward.

For those that have read *Vikings: The Truth about Lagertha and Ragnar* will already see a difference between names according to different historical tomes. In the previous book, Siward was used over Sigurd because that was the common spelling for the *Gesta Danorum*, the manuscript containing Lagertha's story. Whereas, in this book, Sigurd has been used as the common spelling because that is, by far, the most common spelling among the various sags involving Aslaug and Ragnar.

Then, to add even more dimension, one needs to be aware that there are several characters within Viking history that have the same name. Once again, Sigurd is an excellent example of this. Not only was Sigurd Aslaug's father, but there are many Sigurd's in Ragnar's lineage as well. Sigurd was Ragnar's grandfather, but Ragnar's father was also called Sigurd. In addition, traditionally, Ragnar is known to have a son, Sigurd. Therefore, depending on which translation you might be reading, you could encounter many characters all with the same name. In addition, sometimes, it is very hard to interpret from the original source just who the author might be talking about.

Another factor to consider is, in regard to the written word, the Vikings did not record their history and lore like the Christians did, therefore it is difficult to find many sources from the Viking era that are written down. The Vikings culture was handed down orally and, besides the runes, there was no written language. Most of the Viking sagas have originated for poems and oral retellings, meaning it is unclear how the stories originally began and how much has changed over time with each generation of retellings. However, there are a few sources from territories associated with the Vikings, for example, the Icelandic sagas.

Another factor to consider is, in regard to the written word, the Vikings did not record their history and lore like the Christians did, therefore it is difficult to find many sources from the Viking era that are written down by the people involved in the stories. Instead, these tales have often been recorded by Christians, which may lead to bias against the pagan Vikings as a result. However, there are a few sources from territories associated with the Vikings, for example, the Icelandic sagas.

Another obstacle involved with the written lore of the Vikings as recorded by Viking and non-Viking sources alike is the fact these tales were not written down until after the events occurred. Viking culture and traditions were handed down orally and, besides the runes, there was no written language. Most of the Viking sagas have originated for poems and oral retellings, meaning it is unclear how the stories originally began and how much has changed over time with each generation of retellings. In some cases, the tales of the Vikings were written down two hundred years, or more, after the events took place. As a result of this, the Viking sagas need to be read as other myths and legends are in that these stories might vary considerably from the original tale. While it is fantastic someone took the time to record the feats of the Vikings, once again, it is impossible to gauge how much these stories may have changed and evolved prior to them being chronicled.

Along with the time frame, many of the sagas, when finally recorded, used various sources. One author might use several different versions of the one saga, told to them by people who have their own interpretation. The author must then decide which to use in their written one. Sometimes an author might pick their favourite version. Alternatively, they might blend parts of each account together to create their own adaptation of the saga.

This can account for many of the fragments of sagas involving Ragnar Lodbrok. In Saxo's *Gesta Danorum*, Ragnar is seen to have three different wives. The story involving his marriage to Aslaug appears disjointed and, at one point, it is unclear if the children normally associated with Aslaug and Ragnar have, instead, been placed as Thora and Ragnar's children. This can be attributed to the fact Ragnar's story comes in many varied fragments. Saxo may have used some of these fragments, either as we know them today, or earlier, or even subsequently lost, versions of Ragnar's tale. As a result of this, Saxo has placed a moment in a battle where Iwar is only seven years old, but Lagertha's son, Fridleif, is much older. If Saxo's timeline is to be taken at face value, however, it is likely Aslaug and Ragnar were married prior to Lagertha and Ragnar. Which is the true story of Ragnar? It is likely impossible to determine based on the fragments that remain of Ragnar's sagas.

On top of this, the reader also needs to be aware that each saga, besides being a possible blend of different versions of the one story, could also be a blend of historical fact and poetic interpretation. As Ben Waggoner points out, there is also the argument that some of these saga stories have been borrowed from sources outside of the Norse culture that are as varied as Geoffrey of Monmouth's *History of the Kings of Britain*, the bible, and various folk legends from places including Ireland and India.[3]

Regardless of when these stories were written down, or how accurate they really are, they are now the only historical

---

[3] Waggoner, B. (2009). *The Sagas of Ragnar Lodbrok*. Connecticut: The Troth, p. xv.

sources available for the Viking Age. Therefore, when trying to unravel the events that took place during this time, these stories and sagas are one of the tools used. While historians use them to unravel the past, they are also cautious in the knowledge that many of these stories are steeped in hearsay and have evolved over time to become the stories we now know. In some cases, over various sources, there appears to be overlapping of events and different versions of stories that could indicate these events did occur, but were written down by different sources according to the local knowledge of each event or the writer's interpretation of it. While this can be confusing to those trying to unravel the truth, it does also add a certain level of authenticity to a tale if it is recorded in different sources, regardless of the differences contained within the stories. The authenticity then comes from the shared parts of the different versions.

So, what are these historical sources?

The following is a list of some of the historical manuscripts used in relation to unravelling the history of Aslaug and Ragnar that you might want to peruse. This is by no means a concise or complete reading list on the Vikings, merely a starting point based on the stories involving Ragnar Lodbrok.

Gesta Danorum by Saxo Grammaticus.

Historically, this set of sixteen books, also known as the *History of the Danes*, were written some time before 1208. It is unclear when the completion date was however. The first nine books in this series consist of Old Norse mythology. The remainder deal with medieval history. Only four fragments still exist of the original manuscripts: the Angers

Fragment, Lassen Fragment, Kall-Rasmussen Fragment and Plesner Fragment. However, it is only the Angers Fragment that can be attributed to having Saxo's handwriting. Complete later editions of these works date from 1275. Interesting to note is the fact William Shakespeare based his play, *Hamlet*, on a story from the *Gesta Danorum* about Amleth, the Prince of Denmark.

Saxo Grammaticus was a Danish scholar who was encouraged to write the history of the Danes by Absalon, Archbishop of Lund. Some of the *Gesta Danorum* was written in accordance with old Icelandic sagas as well as the parts of history the Archbishop was directly involved with. At times, his religious bias is found within the *Gesta Danorum*, adding further weight to the fact it might not be truly representative of the original sagas.

While this manuscript is not used to explore Aslaug's history, it contains many of Ragnar's stories that crossover with some of Aslaug's story in other books. Therefore, readers can use the *Gesta Danorum* to compare various versions of Ragnar's tales.

The Prose Edda by Snorri Sturluson.

Also called *Snorri's Edda*, *Younger Edda*, or, simply, *Edda*, is a collection of works written by Snorri in Iceland in the early 13th century (estimated sometime around 1220). This means this source is likely more biased toward Viking events, than English or Christian sources. While not necessarily more accurate, it is certainly more sympathetic to the Vikings, their culture and beliefs.

Codex Regius

The *Codex Regius* is thought to have been written sometime in the 1270s. However, historically, it is not until 1643 when the book became more commonly known. Originally, when *The Prose Edda* was the only Edda available, some scholars suggested there was an older body of works containing the full versions of the pagan poems Snorri quoted. When the *Codex Regius* was discovered, many scholars saw this as proof of the original speculation.

The *Codex Regius* and the *Poetic Edda* have been used interchangeably at times, leading to some confusion to those who are starting out in their endeavour to learn about the history of the Vikings. Others prefer to cite the *Codex Regius* as the original source of the *Poetic Edda*. The two have been included separately in this instance to let the reader know when they come across mentions of these tomes they are often in reference to the same, or similar, manuscript.

The Poetic Edda

This body of work is likely based on the *Codex Regius* and there is some evidence to suggest this work could also be called the *Elder Edda* in placement of the *Codex Regius*. As stated above, *The Poetic Edda* and the *Codex Regius* are considered interchangeable, so, if you come across people talking about either sources and they sound surprisingly similar, this is the reason for it.

The Sagas

The sagas usually refer to a collection of Icelandic works

that were written down largely in the 12th through to the 14th centuries, although, sometimes people will describe all sources about the Viking tales as "the sagas." Once again, the Icelandic sagas are stories based on much older tales regarding the migration period during the 5th and 6th centuries and could be considered romanticised versions of the original tales. According to the website, All Scandinavia (allscandinavia.com/icelandsagas), there are about forty sagas in total, ranging in length from a few pages up to 400 pages.

Some of these sagas have been broken up and published under various sources. The *Saga of the Volsungs*, also known as the *Volsunga saga*, is a selection based directly on the Volsung clan that included such characters as Sigurd and Brynhild, the parents of Ragnar's wife, Aslaug.

The *Saga of Ragnar Lodbrok* is considered a sequel to the *Saga of the Volsungs* although it is not usually included in modern day editions of this book. It tells of Ragnar's marriages to Thora and Aslaug as well as the feats of his sons. The *Saga of Ragnar Lodbrok* also deals with his death at the hands of King Ælla.

It should also be mentioned here that "saga" and "tale" are interchangeable within Ragnar's stories. The *Saga of Ragnar Lodbrok* and the *Saga of Ragnar's Sons* are also known as the *Tale of Ragnar Lodbrok* and the *Tale of Ragnar's Sons*. This can lead to confusion when reading about the sagas for the first time as the error can be made that there are four sagas involving Ragnar rather than just two. I have chosen to use the term "saga" throughout this book.

Heimskringla

Also known as *The Lives of the Norse Kings*, this book was

written by Snorri Sturluson in Iceland in the early 13th century (estimated sometime around 1230). This book is a collection of sagas about the Norwegian kings dating from the early Swedish Yngling dynasty through to Harald Fairhair's rule in the 9th century and ending with the death of Eystein Meyla in 1177. It is unclear exactly which sources Snorri used to write this book, but the suggestion is that many stories came from older skaldic poems and earlier kings' sagas. Snorri also lists the now lost work of *Hryggjarstkki* as one of his sources.

Anglo Saxon Chronicle

This chronicle was written sometime late in the 9th century and was being actively updated as late as 1154. This makes it, surprisingly, a fairly accurate source for some events involving the Vikings due to the fact it is, at times, written quite close to actual events as they occur. It is likely this document was originally written in Wessex, England during the reign of Alfred the Great, a man who was directly involved with the Vikings and their conquests. Alfred is usually credited as one of the authors of this document.

While this is an English source, according to Hilda Ellis Davidson, "certain scholars in recent years have come to accept at least part of Ragnar's story as based on historical fact."[4] As a result, the *Anglo Saxon Chronicle* can be considered a source in regards to Ragnar Lodbrok.

---

[4] Saxo Grammaticus (1980) [1979]. Davidson, Hilda Roderick Ellis, ed. Gesta Danorum [Saxo Grammaticus: The history of the Danes: books I–IX]. 1 & 2. Translated by Peter Fisher. Cambridge: D. S. Brewer. Chapter introduction commentaries. ISBN 978-0-85991-502-1. p. 277

ᚠ

As you can see, these sources occur around the time of the Viking era, however, are not usually sources from the early stages of it. While they are some of the only sources known on the Viking era, it must be noted that there may be a level of both bias and error in these sources along with the truth. Nevertheless, without these sources, there would be none of the myths and legends about the Vikings we know of today. Therefore, it is these sources that will be used to delve into the truth behind the Viking characters and the people around them.

THE MYTH OF ASLAUG

SPOILER ALERT: This section contains spoilers about History Channel's *Vikings*, in particular, Season 4.

The myth of Aslaug has evolved over the years and, today, many people will know her as the second wife of Ragnar Lothbrok in the History Channel series, *Vikings*. This character caused conflict between Ragnar and Lagertha after a night of passion between Aslaug and Ragnar resulted in her pregnancy. This led to Lagertha leaving Ragnar and many viewers of the show took Lagertha's side. However, there is much more to Aslaug's legacy than just that of a husband stealer.

Aslaug was born into the Volsung line, a prestigious family that included her famous parents, Sigurd and Brynhild. *Saga of the Volsungs* tells the rise and spectacular fall of this famous clan. It places Aslaug in an esteemed role, even if her saga places her as a peasant at certain points. While she may have been born into an impressive position, when her parents fell, her foster father, Heimir, whisked her away into obscurity. The *Saga of Ragnar Lodbrok* explains this story in great detail from the time of the death of her parents, how she met Ragnar, and through their marriage. However, this saga also gives a little information about her life after Ragnar's death.

While the *Saga of the Volsungs* doesn't spend much time on Aslaug's story, other than to note her conception, it is a valuable source to find out how her world was shaped by the behaviour of her parents. It was because of their bitter squabbling and fighting leading to their deaths that Aslaug ended up the way she did, hidden away from the world as Heimir was fearful that she too would be killed in retribution for the acts of her parents. And so, the secret of her identity is kept hidden until Aslaug is much older and she has no other choice but to reveal her true status or run the risk of losing Ragnar to another woman.

Fans History Channel's *Vikings* often speak of Aslaug in a derogatory manner. In the television series, Aslaug is seen as cold and manipulative to those around her. By the end of their relationship, her and Ragnar are distant and there is often an open show of contempt for each other.

The sagas tell a different story though. The *Saga of Ragnar Lodbrok* shows a relationship that developed after the death of his first wife, Thora. Lagertha is not known in this story, so there is no husband stealing here. In fact, Aslaug and Lagertha never come into any contact in the sagas. Instead, Ragnar woos Aslaug according to her direction and they marry soon after.

There is some confusion pertaining to the division of children between Aslaug and Thora's in Lagertha's tale in the *Gesta Danorum*, however. The author of this book, Saxo Grammaticus, attributes many of Aslaug's children to Thora, which is most likely incorrect as it is the only place these children are cited as being Thora's and not Aslaug's. Although, the *Gesta Danorum* has been cited as one of the sources for the *Saga of Ragnar Lodbrok*, which also mentions Aslaug. So, when looking at this source, it needs to noted that the mention of Aslaug's children in the *Gesta Danorum* could have been incorrect or embellished. In *Vikings: The Truth about Lagertha and Ragnar*, I noted that there appeared to be some sort of discrepancy in regard to Thora's children as she is listed as having two sons to Ragnar. However, four other children are also listed here. These children are usually attributed as being Aslaug's children to Ragnar. Even though the *Gesta Danorum* may be the source for the *Saga of Ragnar Lodbrok*, the general consensus from historians is that the *Gesta Danorum* is erroneous and it is potentially a transcription error or the children are incorrectly recorded by Saxo.

Both the *Saga of Ragnar Lodbrok* and the *Gesta Danorum* were written sometime in the 13th century. However, the *Gesta Danorum* was written very early on in the 13th century, likely before 1208. The *Saga of Ragnar Lodbrok* immediately follows the *Saga of the Volsungs* in the original manuscript although, today, it is usually not included with the English translation. However, the *Saga of the Volsungs* was written down late in the 13th century. The story of Ragnar and Thora overlap in both of these stories.

There is an earlier story that also mentions some of the deeds mentioned in the above two sources. The *Krakumal*, also known as Ragnar's death song, tells of his tales. This skaldic poem is supposed to be the words spoken by Ragnar as he lay dying in King Aelle's snake pit. This poem was first written down in the 12th century and most likely recorded in the Scottish islands. While it doesn't mention Aslaug, it does mention Thora's story, which occurs directly prior to Aslaug's in the *Saga of Ragnar Lodbrok*, indicating this event could have occurred in some capacity.

There may have been some question over whether Lagertha was a real Viking figure; however, it seems likely that Aslaug's story occurred within the Viking Age. She is established as belonging to the Volsung clan, which places her in a timeframe within the Viking Age. While there is much conjecture as to how accurate the Viking sagas are, they are the only written source for the Viking Age, so must be considered as such.

For those trying to track Aslaug's story using English translations, it is an arduous task. Many of the stories involving Aslaug are frequently found in their original languages and readers have to turn to essays on the sources or look at modern translations. However, most of Aslaug's story can be found in the modern translation by Ben Waggoner called *The Sagas of Ragnar Lodbrok*. This book includes translations of the *Saga of Ragnar Lodbrok*, the *List of Swedish Kings*, and the *Saga of Ragnar's Sons*, all of which mention Aslaug's story. Aslaug is also mentioned in *Skaldskaparmal*, which is a section of Snorri Sturluson's *Edda*. A very brief mention of her conception is noted in the *Saga of the Volsungs*.

As far as dating these tomes, once again, most were recorded in the 13th century, but their ages vary from early and right through until late in the century. This gives a board range of time for them to be written, as much as eighty to one hundred years. So, on top of the fact they were recorded as much as two hundred years after the events, some of these sources have drawn from other sources, such as the *Gesta Danorum*, making these stories a melting pot of truth and fiction alike.

However, some truths can be gleaned from the stories. As they overlap, they create common areas that historians more readily conclude is based on fact. If various sources say the same thing, then it seems more likely this event actually happened. Once again, though, many of these stories evolved from oral traditions, so there is no indication at all as to how accurate any of it really is.

This is how many stories of characters like Aslaug have changed and evolved over the years. So, when shows like History Channel's *Vikings* make reference to Aslaug, these references are usually rooted in some sort of saga truth. For although there are overlapping parts of Aslaug's story across the sources, some parts are quite different, or have alternative explanations for events, which means people can pick and choose how to tell her story.

Of course, this led to having to make some creative choices when writing the fictional part of this book. Mostly, Aslaug's tale remains somewhat similar between tellings. However, there has been some room for plot devices at points. As a result of this, I have always chosen to follow the storyline that most fits within the telling of her tale here. Overall, though, I have chosen to tell Aslaug's tale from the *Saga of Ragnar Lodbrok* as this is the most detailed saga involving her story.

Along with there being several versions of Aslaug's story, she also had many different names. While most of the Viking sagas have names that change between documents, Aslaug's name also changes within her story. Initially, she is born as Aslaug and known by that name after her parents die and her foster father, Heimir, takes responsibility for her. He dresses himself as a beggar and hides Aslaug in his harp cover. Together, they travel around the countryside, Aslaug hidden away from the world, and the once noble Heimir, begging for food to get by. Nevertheless, this was the price he was happy to pay to see Aslaug stay safe.

After some time, he came to meet Grima and Aki. Grima immediately suspects Heimir is more than just a lowly beggar and plots with her husband, Aki, to kill Heimir so they can take his riches for their own.

Once Aki murders Heimir, Aslaug is discovered. While Aki is concerned that they have just caused more trouble than it was actually worth, Grima sees Aslaug as the perfect slave for them. She cuts Aslaug's hair, dresses her in rags, and renames her after her mother: Kraka. A name by which Aslaug is known by for a long time after that.

In fact, Ragnar first knows Aslaug by this name. He first meets Aslaug—as Kraka—after his wife, Thora, had died. Taking himself and his grief across the waters, he goes raiding. When he and his crew stop at Spangareid to bake, his men burn the bread they are cooking after witnessing Kraka and her stunning beauty. Of course, Kraka had seen them coming and had bathed and made herself presentable before coming across them in earnest.

The men return to Ragnar's ship and have to explain why they burnt the bread. Ragnar is immediately intrigued and pursues this woman, assuming she could never be as beautiful as his men have said, thinking, instead, that they were just trying to get out of a sticky situation with their leader.

Ragnar arranges a meeting with Kraka and, for fans of History Channel's *Vikings*, this part of Aslaug's tale in the television show is correct. He asks of her the following.

> "If this young maiden seems as lovely to you as has been reported, ask her to come meet me, and I will meet with her; I want her to be mine. But I want for her to be neither clad nor unclad, neither sated nor hungry, and for her not to come alone, yet no one may come with her."[5]

It is love at first sight for Ragnar when he lays eyes on Kraka and he immediately begins to woo her. Kraka, however, plays hard to get and Ragnar is drawn into her trap. While Kraka may not have been intentionally laying a trap to snare herself a king, it is possible she was trying to attract a man who could get her out of the horrible living conditions with Grima and Aki. But, as luck should have it, she happened upon Ragnar and he did not care that she was a peasant. This is something that was usually not commonly acceptable within Viking culture at the time. It was something that would come back to haunt the couple much later on, though.

Aslaug sends Ragnar away for a time, using the excuse that he would find someone much more suitable by means of a higher standing, than her in his travels. Ragnar is still convinced Kraka is the woman for him and insists he will return as soon as he has visited Norway.

Ragnar leaves, asking her to accept the gift of one of his ex-wife's shirts. Kraka refuses to take it, stating that she is too common to wear something of such finery. However, there is likely an ulterior motive to Ragnar wanting Kraka to wear Thora's shirt. According to Ben Waggoner, a Faeroese ballad called *Ragnars kvadi* tells of Thora prophesising she would die and that "her clothes will fit Ragnar's next wife perfectly."[6]

Ragnar does return to Kraka after his trip to Norway. He professes his love to her and Kraka accepts his marriage proposal. She then tells Grima and Aki that she knows they murdered her foster father and that she is leaving with

[5] Waggoner, B. (2009). *The Sagas of Ragnar Lodbrok*. Connecticut: The Troth, p. 9.

[6] Waggoner, B. (2009). *The Sagas of Ragnar Lodbrok*. Connecticut: The Troth, p. 99.

Ragnar. She also tells them that she will not have them killed because they did raise her and it is a courtesy she must respect. However, she curses them thusly.

> "I know that you killed Heimir, my foster-father, and I want to pay back no one but you. For the sake of the long time that I have lived with you two, I will not do you any harm—but I now pronounce that each day will be worse for you than those that have passed, and your last day will be the worst. Now we are parted."

Kraka then leaves with Ragnar and they wed once they return to his kingdom. Years go by after that and Kraka bears many sons to Ragnar. They appear to be very happy together and there is no indication their marriage was unhappy as is suggested in History Channel's *Vikings*.

However, there seems to be the assumption by at least some of those surrounding Ragnar that their king had married beneath himself. There is no open conversation about this until Ragnar is visiting with a fellow king, and friend, Eystein. Kraka is at home, pregnant with another of their children during this meeting. During a night where a lot of alcohol is consumed, some of Ragnar's men convince him that he should marry Eystein's daughter, Ingibjorg, who is a much more fitting bride than the commoner, Kraka. King Eystein is in agreeance and Ragnar becomes betrothed to Ingibjorg. It is mentioned that the betrothal would last for some time, possibly suggesting that Ingibjorg was too young to be married yet. Or, perhaps, so Ragnar could go home and dispose of his current wife.

There is no indication in the text that Ragnar wants to put

Kraka aside. In fact, when they all return home, Ragnar implores his men keep silent about his betrothal to Ingibjorg. He threatens their very lives in order to keep them quiet.

It is all for nought, though. Kraka, who is often said to be a magical volva—or one who can see things even though she isn't present, confronts Ragnar immediately. She begs of him not to marry Ingibjorg and finally reveals her true identity.

Ragnar is not sure he believes her at first but Aslaug insists Ragnar wait until their child is born. She prophesises that this child will be a boy and he will bear the image of a snake in his eye. Aslaug tells Ragnar that if their child is not born this way then he is free to leave her and marry Ingibjorg.

Of course, what Aslaug says comes to be true, and this is how their son, Sigurd becomes known as Sigurd Snake-in-the-Eye. This event proves that what Aslaug said about her heritage is correct and her true name is finally revealed to everyone. At this point, most seem happy to now accept the common Kraka as the noble Aslaug. There are further complications with Ragnar and Eystein but, for now, Ragnar and Aslaug can go back to be happy again.

However, Aslaug goes by one final name in her sagas: Randalin. This is the name she uses when she takes the helm as commander of Ivar's land forces when they fight against Eystein. After this event, she is known as Randalin and not Aslaug. However, for the sake of the fictional retelling of her story, I have not used this name since it bears no relevance to the story such as Kraka did.

There is also some who believe that Aslaug goes by a fourth name. As I discuss in *Ragnar and the Women Who Loved Him*, in the *Gesta Danorum*, a woman called Swanloga is mentioned as also being a wife of Ragnar.

> "He besought the aid of the brothers Biorn, Fridleif, and Ragbard (for Ragnald, Hwitserk, and Erik, his sons by Swanloga, had not yet reached the age of bearing arms), and went to Sweden."[7]

Because some of these sons are known to be Aslaug's children in other sagas, the assumption could be made that Swanloga and Aslaug are the same women.

However, later on in the text, it is also mentioned that Swanloga dies in much the same way as Thora does. So, it seems just as likely Swanloga and Thora are the same woman at this point. As a result, it is hard to see whom Saxo meant in the *Gesta Danorum*, especially since Swanloga is only ever mentioned in two brief passages.

So, with all these names, is it possible Aslaug's story is actually about many different women? It certainly could be a mash up of a multitude of different women's stories. However, scholars mostly believe that this is the one story about a singular woman.

While Aslaug's saga is appealing outright, for many people the fact that she was the mother of so many famous Vikings is what draws them in to her story. In History Channel's *Vikings*, Bjorn Ironside is the son of Lagertha. However, in the sagas, Aslaug is his mother. Along with Bjorn, Ivar the Boneless, Hvitserk, Ubbe, and Sigurd Snake-in-the-Eye are all considered children of Aslaug.

Bjorn is known to have become a legendary king of Sweden and the head of the Munso dynasty. In fact, it is said that his remains still reside in a barrow on Munso Island,

---

[7] Grammaticus, S. (2016). *The Danish History Books I-X.* [e-book]. Perennial Press. Available through: <https://www.amazon.com/Danish-History-Books-I-IX-ebook/dp/B01BRM2VFQ/> [Accessed: 2017].

which is a part of the Ekero Municipality in Sweden today.

Just like in the television series, Bjorn led a Viking raid into the Mediterranean. He was also known to have led many successful raids in France and Italy; one of which fans of the television series will know.

While Ragnar was credited with a raid in Paris that saw him fake his own death in order to get inside the fortified city, it was, in fact, Bjorn who used this devious plan—and to infiltrate the Italian city of Luni. Although, at the time, he thought they were invading Rome. Using the Christian faith against them, Bjorn pretended to have had a deathbed conversion to Christianity and was seeking to now be buried in holy ground. Once inside, his band of men hacked through the gates and let the remaining Viking army inside.

However, it is Ivar the Boneless that is usually considered the most famous of Ragnar and Aslaug's sons. If not the most famous, he is certainly the most complexing.

While historians believe he existed in some capacity and created a fantastical legacy, it is his name that causes the most confusion. Most people refer to him as Ivar the Boneless, and assume he had some sort of illness that made his legs unusable but it is possible this translation of his name is incorrect. Some of his other references and alterations on his moniker can give some clues that his common name of Ivar the Boneless might be an alliteration.

Ivar the Despicable and Ivar the Hated both indicate Ivar was not very well liked. However, it is the translation of the original word used to describe Ivar that indicates a mistake might have been made to call him "boneless." Throughout the sagas, Ivar is known to be quite ruthless, hence the possibility of this title.

However, another reason to explain why Ivar was known

as "boneless" comes down to a mistake in translation. Clare Downham from the University of Liverpool explained in the History Channel documentary, *Real Vikings*, that Ivar's given moniker, when translated from Latin, could have been erroneously mixed up with a word that translates to "despicable" and not "boneless" as these Latin words are very similar.

There are other explanations for Ivar's name as well. Some suspect "boneless" could be a reference to his dexterity and flexibility on the battlefield as there are references to him being incredibly nimble and lucky within his stories. The Old Norse poem, *Háttalykill inn forni*, sees Ivar the Boneless being described as having amazing flexibility, hence the reference to him appearing to be like he has no bones.

Along with this alternative description of Ivar the Boneless, there is one other possibility to explain Ivar's nickname: impotency. Considering the general consensus is that Ivar did not father any children, this explanation could also be possible. Plus, there is evidence within the sagas that this might be the case thanks to a reference in the *Saga of Ragnar Lodbrok* that explains Ivar by saying he had "no lust nor love in him."[8]

But, these explanations do not explain away the fact that Ivar's birth story involves Aslaug stating to Ragnar that their son would be born a cripple if they had sex on their wedding night, instead of waiting for three days to pass. There are also references within his sagas that describe Ivar's impediment. So, for those reading the sagas, they must make up their own mind as to whether Ivar was really a cripple or not.

Sigurd Snake-in-the-Eye is another of Aslaug's famous

---

[8] Waggoner, B. (2009). *The Sagas of Ragnar Lodbrok*. Connecticut: The Troth, p. 70.

sons. While history Channel's *Vikings* saw the premature death of Sigurd in the Season 4 finale, Sigurd's tale is much greater than that as portrayed in the television series.

As mentioned previously, Sigurd got his name when born and this eye deformity helped Kraka prove she was Aslaug. Sigurd was then named after his grandfather, Aslaug's father, the famous dragon slayer.

Along with this, he also grew up to be a success in the Viking world. When he was very young, Sigurd Snake-in-the-Eye accompanied Ragnar on a trip to the Hellespont, a natural strait of water in north-western Turkey.

According to the *Saga of Ragnar Lodbrok*, when his father died, Sigurd inherited the following lands: Zealand, Scania, Halland, the Danish islands, and Viken. He then married Blaeja, the daughter of King Aelle. They had four children and Sigurd went on to take Halfdan's lead as the King of Denmark after he died around 877. One of Sigurd's daughter's, Ragnhild, is said to be the mother of Harald Fairhair (known as King Harald Finehair in the television series), who went on to become the first ruler of the united Norway.

Along with these sons, Aslaug also bore Hvitserk and Ubbe. There is some confusion between these two sons, in both existence and to whom they actually belong.

Hvitserk only appears in the *Saga of Ragnar's Sons*. He is also never mentioned in any stories that list Halfdan as a son of Ragnar, so the general assumption is that these names are interchangeable and only one person exists here. Hvitserk was known to be one of the leaders of the Great Heathen Army.

While Ubbe is quite often listed as one of Aslaug's sons, Ubbe may have also been the son of one of Ragnar's lovers.

In the *Gesta Danorum*, an unnamed woman is supposed to be the mother of Ubbe. Ragnar pursued her and managed to bed her even though she was considered beneath his standing. Later, when Ubbe is grown up, he is said to have loved his mother but despised his father. The reason for this is because his mother managed to ensnare a man above her standing but his father, Ragnar, fell below his station. Once again, it is a reference to how standing was considered important in Viking culture and signifies how amazing it was that Ragnar married Kraka when he considered her a commoner and people actually accepted this marriage at the start before her true identity was revealed.

While not her own son, a mention needs to be made of one of Ragnar's sons, Eirik (also known as Erik or Eric). This child is one of Thora's children and raised as a stepchild by Aslaug after the death of Thora and Aslaug's subsequent marriage to Ragnar.

In Ben Waggoner's interpretation of the *Sagas of Ragnar Lodbrok*, it is noted that Aslaug became so distressed when hearing the news about the death of Eirik that she cried bloody tears. Not long after receiving this information, she was also told that one of her own sons, Rognvald, had perished. It is noted "that news didn't affect her much."[9] Instead, she talks of Rognvald's warrior skills and how she considers him a fine son rather than bemoaning his death in the way she did with Eirik.

There is no written indication that Aslaug and Eirik had anything more than a mother and stepson relationship. However, over the years, people have questioned whether the pair was involved with each other more than they should be.

---

[9] Waggoner, B. (2009). *The Sagas of Ragnar Lodbrok*. Connecticut: The Troth, p. 21.

Once again, the sagas being scant on information, readers will have to come to their own conclusions here.

In spite of this questionable relationship with one of her stepchildren, her story suggests just how much she favoured her husband. Even though Ragnar became betrothed to Ingibjorg, she still stood by him, insisting he stay with her once her identity was exposed.

The couple lived a long life together and, at the end, when Ragnar made his final voyage to England, Aslaug was distraught enough to try to convince him to stay. Thanks to a premonition, she advised Ragnar that it would be careless to make such a perilous journey. However, Ragnar insisted on making his impossible trip to England. This was in an effort to make himself more renowned than his sons who were now considered more famous than Ragnar. As a result of this, Aslaug insisted on making Ragnar a magical shirt. This shirt would help to protect him from being killed or maimed, making sure weapons were turned away from him and not causing him any injury. Aslaug insisted Ragnar wear this shirt for the entire time he travelled to England, and also while he was there. When he left, she was said to be visibly distressed at his leaving.

Aslaug is mentioned after Ragnar's death. After her sons revenge the death of their father by King Aelle, it is noted that Aslaug (known as Randalin) is now an old woman. There is evidence in the sagas that she outlived her son, Hvitserk. However, her death is never recorded.

WHO WERE THE MAGICAL VOLVAS?

It is often referenced that Aslaug is a volva (or völva). But, what is this?

A volva is, essentially, a female magical shaman or seer. There are many times during Aslaug's stories that see her knowing things she shouldn't know that helps support this idea.

The term volva originates from Old Norse and translates into "wand carrier" or "carrier of a magic staff." The term is often associated with seidhr, another term that relates to those who practise magic. Both of these terms are often used to describe women who specialise in being able to see into the future or events they have not been made privy to under normal circumstances.

To be a volva or seidhr was something usually only assigned to females in the Viking world, unlike the Seer who is male in History Channel's *Vikings*. For many Vikings, if a male was called a volva or seidhr it was considered somewhat effeminate in manner. In many Norse cultures the unmanliness associated with being known as a volva or seidhr when you were male in orientation was considered a slur when used in the masculine.

However, no such connotations occurred in reverse when a female was known as a volva. The opposite seems to come into play with female seers considered an esteemed position to hold.

As to be expected with being a volva, Aslaug seems to know many things beyond normal expectation within her stories. She predicts Ivar will be born with a disability if she and Ragnar consummate their marriage immediately after their wedding. Aslaug also tells Ragnar that their last son will be born with what appears to be the image of a snake in his eye and this will prove her identity when it is questioned.

However, there are other instances. When Ragnar becomes betrothed to King Eystein's daughter, Ingibjorg (also known as Borghild in the *Saga of Ragnar's Sons*), she knows of this event even before Ragnar has returned. She questions Ragnar about what happened when he visited the king and when Ragnar insists there was no news to report, she goes on to tell him what she knows. Aslaug asserts she knows of his betrothal thanks to three birds she had spy on him.

> "You must have seen three birds were sitting in a tree next to you. They told me this news."[10]

She then goes on to reveal her true identity to Ragnar and decrees he wait until after the birth of their child is born as proof that she is really Aslaug of the Volsung clan.

Aslaug also knows something will happen to Ragnar when he plans his final trip to England. She tries to get him to terminate the trip but, when this doesn't work, she makes him a magical shirt. As Ragnar prepares to leave on this voyage, Aslaug presents him with the shirt and offers the following verse.

> "Stitched and seamed nowhere,
> This long shirt I give you;
> Out of hoar-grey hair-strands,
> With a high heart, I wove it.

---

[10] Waggoner, B. (2009). *The Sagas of Ragnar Lodbrok*. Connecticut: The Troth, p. 15.

No wound will be bloody,
Nor will weapons bite you
If you have this hallowed tunic,
Made holy by the gods."[11]

Within the Viking sagas, magic is often represented, interwoven in with the stories of the gods that resided in a place called Asgard, as well as their daily lives in the human plane of Midgard. To them, offering to the gods, magic, and everyday living were all combined, all were real. So, it makes sense that there are characters within the Viking sagas— especially women—who were magical. Men, on the other hand, were not usually considered magical like women were, although, characters whom are hidden gods do sometimes exist.

Along with Aslaug being considered a volva, her mother was also known to have been a magical woman. Brynhildr is often called a valkyrie. These magical women are said to descend onto the battlefield and select those worthy of being taken away to Valhalla.

At the end of time when an event called Ragnarok is meant to occur, these mighty warriors will be summoned in a battle between the gods that will result in the near eradication of life on earth—the gods included. The valkyries only take the most fearsome and skilled warriors. Therefore, to die in battle was considered a great honour to a Viking as it meant their position in Valhalla and the Ragnarok event was confirmed. Traditionally, the valkyries only chose half of the fallen; the other half went to the goddess Freya.

While valkyries were usually considered to reside away from humans, there are stories that tell of valkyries who have slept with men or fallen in love with them for a time. So, to have Aslaug's mother identified as a valkyrie, yet also being married to the human Sigurd, is not as contradictory as first

---

[11] Waggoner, B. (2009). *The Sagas of Ragnar Lodbrok*. Connecticut: The Troth, p. 29.

thought. It is also a way to explain why the human Aslaug could be considered a volva.

THE MYTH OF RAGNAR

The legend involving Ragnar Lodbrok is a messy, murky one. It is unclear exactly where Ragnar existed, if he was an amalgamation of several men known as Ragnar (or variants on that name), or merely a figment of the mythic parts of the sagas.

Regardless, Ragnar Lothbrok is also known as; Ragnar Lodbrok, Ragnar Lodbrog, Ragnar "Lodbrok" Sigurdsson or Ragnar Sigurdsson. Sigurdsson literally translates to the son of Sigurd. In the *Gesta Danorum*, Ragnar has his father listed as Siward Ring, which, is a variant spelling of Sigurd Hring (or, alternatively, Sigurd Ring), and hence where the surname of Sigurdsson has originated from.

It is possible, over the years that Ragnar's deeds have been attributed to several different people. Author of *The Sagas of Ragnar Lodbrok*, Ben Waggoner, lists several different variants on the name, Ragnar, that have been attributed to Ragnar Lodbrok over the years. The *Frankish Chronicles* sees a man called Reginheri being mentioned. The stories attributing Ragnar Lodbrok's raids on Paris can be linked back to this source. Ragnar might also be a man called Raginarius who was given land and a monastery by Charles the Bald in 840. While the sagas involving Ragnar Lodbrok don't specifically place Ragnar in Ireland, there is also evidence in Saxo's *Gesta Danorum* to suggest he could have raided there. It is also possible he could have died there sometime between 852 and 856 thanks to sources such as the Irish chronicles. Another variant on his name that could be attributed to Ragnar is a Norse King called Ragnall. Although, it is possible this person could also be attributed to Reginheri and are not two separate people.

In recent culture, many would know Ragnar as Ragnar Lothbrok in History's *Vikings*. This character started out as a farmer, married to Lagertha, with two children; a girl, Gyda, and a son, Bjorn Ironside.

In the first season, Ragnar decides to buck against the wishes of the Earl of Kattegat and venture into unchartered waters, which turns out to reveal England. Thus begins the first invasion of England, when Ragnar's small fleet attacks the abbey at Lindisfarne, an event that has been historically recorded by English sources although not attributed to Ragnar specifically.

In the television series, this raid is the catalyst needed to catapult Ragnar into becoming the new earl of Kattegat, and, later, a king. This story is a very interesting way to show the first Viking raid and to develop the story of both how the Viking era begins, as well as to introduce how the legend of Ragnar Lodbrok (known in the television series as Ragnar Lothbrok) first began. However, Ragnar's beginnings differ quite significantly in the sagas that relate to his life. It is also highly unlikely the Vikings introduction to England was via a single raid.

In this book, however, I will only be dealing with the story that directly correlates with Ragnar and Aslaug's story. The *Gesta Danorum* does not really address Ragnar's birth, but it does introduce him from a very young age at points. According to the ninth book of the *Gesta Danorum*, Ragnar was not a farmer, or from farming stock. His grandfather was a king, and Ragnar's father was in a position to follow into leadership. Then, as circumstance dictates, Ragnar is proclaimed king when he is very young.

Ragnar's cunning and ability to rally those around him is indicated from a very early age. Before he meets Lagertha at the battle to free the wives of Siward's kin from a life of prostitution, Ragnar had already proven his worth well before he became a man.

Before Ragnar's grandfather Siward became king, another had been vying for the position. Ragnar's father was involved in many disputes in relation to who ruled the lands. In the meantime, locals claimed his son, Ragnar, as the rightful king, hoping this would add more weight to Siward's claim. Ragnar was only a baby at the time, but they anticipated this would draw out those who were sluggish at showing support for Siward and they would, in turn, renew their support.

What ended up happening, though, was retaliation that resulted in Siward's supporters being forced to choose between, as Saxo put it, "shame or peril."

This is when the legend of Ragnar was first born. This name, translated from the Old Norse elements ragin- "counsel" and hari- "army" goes a long way in explaining the myth of Ragnar and how he is known for his way with people.

Being only a boy at the time, he still managed to rally those around him. Those who were at counsel over what to be done had not come to a decision, so Ragnar offered his opinion. Considering the conundrum they were all in, they chose to, at least, hear the boy out. According to Saxo, Ragnar's advice was as follows.

"The short bow shoots its shaft suddenly. Though it may seem the hardihood of a boy that I venture to forestall the speech of the elders, yet I pray you to pardon my errors, and be indulgent to my unripe words. Yet the counsellor of wisdom is not to be spurned, though he seem contemptible; for the teaching of profitable things should be drunk in with an open mind. Now it is shameful that we should be branded as deserters and runaways, but it is just as foolhardy to venture above our strength; and thus there is proved to be equal blame either way. We must, then, pretend to go over to the enemy, but, when a chance comes in our way, we must desert betimes. It will this be better to forestall the wrath of our foe by reigned obedience than, by refusing it, to give him a weapon wherewith to attack us yet more harshly; for if we decline the sway of the stronger, are we not simply turning his arms against our own throat? Intricate devices are often the best nurse of craft. You need cunning to trap a fox."[12]

So, what does all that mean? Ragnar's plan was simple; they would play along until there was a moment when they could attack.

Concerned at the fate of Ragnar if he were to be drawn into the battle, he was sent from Zealand to Norway to be raised. Ragnar's plans, however, were still followed. In the process, though, Siward was mortally wounded and the young Ragnar was now the king proper. Therefore, by this time, Ragnar was still young, but old enough to pursue Lagertha

[12] Grammaticus, Saxo. The Danish History Books I-X. Perennial Press (February 15, 2016). p. 3. ISBN 1468086847

when the King of Sweden killed Siward, the King of Norway.

While Ragnar's tales are great, there is some dispute as to whether Ragnar was just one man, or, even existed at all. Hilda Ellis Davidson notes that book nine of the *Gesta Danorum* may actually be an amalgamation of several events that appear to be contradictory to each other.

Ellis lists the following historical figures that may be considered to fall under some of Ragnar's tales in her commentary on the *Gesta Danorum*:

- King Horik I
- King Reginfrid
- A King of Demark known to have come into conflict with Harald Klak (this could be the Harald mentioned earlier involving the battle where Lagertha triumphed.)
- Reginherus, a person who invaded Paris in the middle of the ninth century
- Rognvald of the Irish Annals
- The father of the Viking leaders who led the Great Heathen Army in 865

Regardless of Ragnar's authenticity or not, the medieval sources involving Ragnar Lodbrok include the following sources:

- Book nine of the *Gesta Danorum*, which is the tale that also covers Lagertha's story
- The *Saga of Ragnar's Sons* also known as the *Ragnarssona þáttr* saga
- The *Saga of Ragnar Lodbrok*, a sequel to the *Volsunga*

saga

- *The Ragnarsdrápa*, which is a fragmented skaldic poem attributed to the 9th-century poet Bragi Boddason
- *The Krákumál*, a 12th-century Icelandic poem which is also known as Ragnar's death-song

Ragnar's time with Lagertha seems short in the *Gesta Danorum*, and, after they parted ways, he continued to do many great deeds. In fact, it wasn't until after he and Lagertha separated, did he obtain the nickname Lodbrok.

In the ninth book of the *Gesta Danorum*, it is explained that Ragnar, became, once again, infatuated with a woman— this time Thora Borgarhjört. Thora was surrounded by dangerous animals and Ragnar tried to kill the beasts in order to gain her father, King Herraud (Herrauðr) of Sweden's, approval in marriage.

The animals he had to battle this time around were dangerous serpents that Thora had raised herself.

Ragnar, being a smart man who was happy to wait patiently, observed many men attempting to kill the animals. From this, he formulated a plan to cover the lower part of his body in thick, shaggy hides that the snakes would not be able to pierce. He also covered these hairy breeches in tar and sand, as added protection.

It was these pants, plus a shield that protected him from the serpents' venom, that allowed Ragnar to get close enough to slay the serpents and win Thora's hand. King Herraud was so impressed – and amused – with Ragnar's hairy pants that he gave Ragnar the nickname, Loðbrók, which translates literally into "Hairy-Breeks" or, more commonly, hairy breeches.

It is said, in the ninth book of the *Gesta Danorum*, that

Ragnar loved Thora dearly. When she died of an unknown, but violent, malady, it caused Ragnar "infinite trouble and distress." Ragnar decided to put this misery to good use and found solace in exercise and hard work.

It was this event that led him to create an army that consisted of those that each family thought were too contemptible or lazy to be of much service to them, be it son or slave. This was something he had tried out to a lesser degree during the battle Lagertha helped him with, employing those considered too old or weak to help him when he wasn't sure his army would be big enough. The army was then used to prove that the "feeblest of the Danish race were better than the strongest men of other nations."

This is also the point in the *Gesta Danorum* when a major timeframe conflict occurs. While Aslaug is never mentioned in the ninth book, her children are. When the children of Ragnar and Thora are listed, they are added to the children of Aslaug's without mentioning who the mother actually is. Other sources, however, credit these children to Ragnar and Aslaug. So, either Ragnar married Aslaug prior to Lagertha, or in between his divorce to her and subsequent marriage to Thora. In the *Gesta Danorum,* however, it seems like Ragnar divorced Lagertha and immediately began his pursuit of Thora.

In fact, the story of Lagertha in the *Gesta Danorum* leads to several conflicts when rewriting it in the modern day. When wanting to tell only Lagertha and Ragnar's love story in the first book in this series, *Vikings: The Truth About Lagertha and Ragnar*, it cannot actually be told without placing all of his wives in the picture.

Aslaug must be explained at some point, and, by effect, how their marriage ended in order to place her child, Siward, in the picture, as he appears, briefly, at the end of Lagertha's story and can, potentially, be used as a catalyst for a reunion between the pair.

While Ragnar is also known by the moniker, Ragnar Lodbrok, it was not until he met Thora did he get this name. The ninth chapter of the *Gesta Danorum* explains how Ragnar, after leaving Lagertha on account of his distrust over he initially setting wild beasts against him, ironically, finds himself battling more beasts to win his next wife's hand. Her father gave Ragnar the nickname, Lodbrok, on account of his snake-resistant pants and the name, much like the tar he used on them, stuck.

So, where does Aslaug fit into all of this?

While Aslaug is never mentioned alongside Lagertha and Thora in the *Gesta Danorum*, she does appear in other places. In the *Saga of Ragnar Lodbrok*, Ragnar first encounters her after the death of his wife, Thora. Many of the events that occur in this story overlap with what Saxo describes in the *Gesta Danorum*, even if Aslaug is omitted. She is also mentioned in the *Saga of Ragnar's Sons*. Once again, some of these stories also cross over as Ragnar's story is explored.

Considering Ragnar got his famous surname because of battling snakes, it is not the last time snakes are involved in his story. The second time they are present, however, is also the last time.

Ragnar Lodbrok meets his end at the hand of King Ælla of Northumbria. Ælla had captured Ragnar and, as punishment for the Viking raids that had occurred on his kingdom, had Ragnar thrown into a pit of venomous snakes.

The death song of Ragnar Lodbrok, the *Krákumál* describes how Ragnar valiantly sung as he died, ready and willing to enter Valhalla after he perished.

"It gladdens me to know that Baldr's father [Odin] makes ready the benches for a banquet. Soon we shall be drinking ale from the curved horns. The champion who comes into Odin's dwelling [Valhalla] does not lament his death. I shall not enter his hall with words of fear upon my lips. The Æsir will welcome me. Death comes without lamenting. Eager am I to depart. The Dísir summon me home, those whom Odin sends for me [Valkyries] from the halls of the Lord of Hosts. Gladly shall I drink ale in the high-seat with the Æsir. The days of my life are ended. I laugh as I die."[13]

Varying sources place this event sometime around 840 through to 865. However, Ragnar's sons avenged his death when their Great Heathen Army attacked in 865 and it is suggested by some sources that Ælla was killed in the battle at York by the Great Heathen Army in 867. Symeon's *Historia Regum Anglorum* gives the date for this battle and Ælla's subsequent death as 21 March, 867. The account is described below.

"In those days, the nation of the Northumbrians had violently expelled from the kingdom the rightful king of their nation, Osbryht by name, and had placed at the head of the kingdom a certain tyrant, named Alla [Ælla]. When the pagans came upon the kingdom, the dissension was allayed by divine counsel and the aid of the nobles. King Osbryht and Alla,

---

[13] Symeon of Durham; J. Stevenson, translator (1855). "The Historical Works of Simeon of Durham". Church Historians of England, volume III, part II. Seeley's. Retrieved 2007-01-27

having united their forces and formed an army, came to the city of York; on their approach the multitude of the shipmen immediately took flight. The Christians, perceiving their flight and terror, found that they themselves were the stronger party. They fought upon each side with much ferocity, and both kings fell. The rest who escaped made peace with the Danes."[14]

In History's *Vikings*, the Viking tradition of killing a foe using the "blood eagle" was shown on Jarl Borg as well as King Ælla. However, it is suggested, historically, this grisly death was reserved for Ælla alone in Ragnar's story.

In the television program, the blood eagle is described as being a form of sacrifice where the person has their back cut open, their ribs also cut, exposing the foe's internal organs. The lungs are then brought out and laid upon the person's back, making what looking like a pair of bloody wings, hence the term, blood eagle. The person undergoing this ordeal is supposed to remain silent during it if they wish to enter Valhalla after death, therefore making their death honourable.

However, there is some dispute as to whether this blood eagle sacrifice actually occurred like this. Once again, there may be a discrepancy in translation that has led to the current day belief of what a blood eagle really is.

The image below certainly makes it appear that the blood eagle was an actual bloody sacrifice. The Stora Hammars I stone from Gotland, Sweden shows a man lying prone while another stand over him with a weapon. Eagles are shown in

[14] Symeonis Dunelmensis Opera et collectanea. Simeon, of Durham, d. ca. 1130; Making of America Project; Hodgson-Hinde, John, 1806-1869. Published 1868

the air above them.

[Image via Sacrificial_scene_on_Hammars_(I).JPG: Berig | Wikimedia Commons | Cropped and Resized | CC-BY-SA-3.0]

Although, in regard to the above image, it has also been interpreted as showing a sacrifice to a god, likely Odin, thanks to the appearance of a raven in the image. Another person is described as hanging from a noose in the top left-hand side of the image.

Therefore, when using sources such as the one above, it is shown, once again, how much interpretation of the situation can alter the perception of what the item originally meant to display.

There are two instances of the blood eagle being performed in the Viking sagas. The *Orkneyinga* saga describes the blood eagle performed on Harald Fairhair's son Halfdan Long-Leg.

> "Einarr made them carve an eagle on his back with a sword, and cut the ribs all from the backbone, and draw the lungs there out, and gave him to Odin for the victory he had won."[15]

---

[15] Dasent, G.W. (1894). "Icelandic Sagas and Other Historical Documents Relating to the Settlements and Dsecents of the Northmen

The other instance in in *Þáttr af Ragnars sonum*. Both times this event occurs to royalty, and both times it is in retaliation for the death of a father.

Þáttr af Ragnars sonum (also known as the *Saga of Ragnar's Sons*) described Ragnar's son, Ivar the Boneless avenging his father's death by performing the blood eagle on Ælla.

> "They caused the bloody eagle to be carved on the back of Ælla, and they cut away all of the ribs from the spine, and then they ripped out his lungs."[16]

Both of these descriptions seem like the blood eagle is a gruesome sacrifice that involves cutting into a person's back. However, there are some who believe these English translations may have been erroneous.

An eleventh-century poet, Sigvatr Þórðarson, in his poem, *Knútsdrápa*[17], depicts Ivar the Boneless performing the blood eagle on Ælla. And it is this poem that can be offered alternate translations on what the blood eagle actually is.

There is some suggestion that either an eagle was used to cut a foe's back, or that the eagle, being a common Viking symbol that meant death or blood, was more symbolic than that.

> "And Ella's back,
> at had the one who dwelt,

---

on the British Isles Vol III - The Orkneyinger's Saga". Rerum Britannicarum Medii Ævi Scriptores, Or, Chronicles and Memorials of Great Britain and Ireland During the Middle Ages. University of Minnesota: Great Britain. Public Record Office. 88 (3): xxvi, 8–9. Retrieved 30 March 2015.

[16] Waggoner, Ben (2009), *The Sagas of Ragnar Lodbrok*, The Troth, ISBN 978-0-578-02138-6

[17] Knútsrápra by Sigvatr Þórðarson, Skaldic Poetry of the Scandinavian Middle Ages

> Ivarr, with eagle,
> York, cut."[18]

The above translation could be an alternative interpretation of a blood eagle according to Roberta Frank in *Viking atrocity and Skaldic verse: The Rite of the Blood-Eagle*.

Saxo also makes mention of the blood eagle in book nine of the *Gesta Danorum*. His description of the blood eagle sacrifice is quite different to current ideas.

> "They ordered the figure of an eagle to be cut in his back, rejoicing to crush their most ruthless roe by marking him with the cruellest of birds. Not satisfied with imprinting a wound in him, they salted the mangled flesh. Thus Ella [Ælla] was done to death, and Bjorn and Siward went back to their own kingdoms."[19]

While Saxo's description is less brutal than hacking through the rib cage and removing Ælla's lungs, it is telling that the wounds were deep enough to cause the death of Ælla.

And so, with the death of Ragnar, and the consequences of his killer described, it is time to conclude this section.

---

[18] Frank, Roberta (1984). "Viking atrocity and Skaldic verse: The Rite of the Blood-Eagle" (PDF). English Historical Review. Oxford Journals. XCIX (CCCXCI): 332–343. doi:10.1093/ehr/XCIX.CCCXCI.332. Retrieved 30 March 2015.

[19]19 Grammaticus, Saxo. The Danish History Books I-X. Perennial Press (February 15, 2016). p. 3. ISBN 1468086847

THE MYTH OF ASLAUG AND RAGNAR

For those being first introduced to the Viking stories surrounding Aslaug, and, in particular, Ragnar, there is the very harsh discovery that Ragnar had many wives and partners. Over the course of the stories involving him, he is acknowledged as having three wives: Lagertha, Thora, and Aslaug. He is also associated with other women including one woman considered beneath his standing in the ninth book of Saxo's *Gesta Danorum*.

However, regardless of whom Ragnar is involved with, all of Ragnar's significant relationships seem to involve some sort of initial trial. As discussed previously, Aslaug insisted Ragnar complete his mission before they could wed.

Then, Lagertha had Ragnar fight beasts to gain her hand in marriage. Ragnar, impressed by her feats on the battlefield, was happy to kill the bear and hound she placed around her home for protection from him, although, he came to regret this event later on in their story. In History Channel's *Vikings*, viewers often consider this relationship as the most significant of Ragnar's unions. By comparison, Aslaug and Ragnar's marriage is considered a failure and, by the time Ragnar leaves for England, it is barely considered a union at all. However, this is unlikely the case according to the sagas.

The sagas see Aslaug and Ragnar's marriage as occurring after the death of Thora and ends with the death of Ragnar in England at the hands of King Aelle. During their marriage there seems to be little conflict, even when Ragnar becomes accidentally betrothed to another woman.

Ragnar also had to battle serpents to gain Thora's hand in

marriage, a similar trial to that of Lagertha's. While Ragnar ended up begrudging the fact Lagertha set wild beasts onto him to win her hand, he never seemed to be angry with Thora about her beasts. Therefore, it could be assumed here that maybe Ragnar and Lagertha's union was not the greatest Viking love story of all time, as indicated in the television series, since he happily killed Thora's snakes and never regretted it. It could also suggest that Ragnar shared a significant relationship with this woman prior to his marriage to Aslaug. However, considering Thora died and then Ragnar married Aslaug, there is little to suggest one relationship was favoured over the other by Ragnar as the sagas are very scant on information in this regard and often don't speak greatly about the characters persuasions and reasoning for what they do.

Once again, while Ragnar was disgruntled at having to fight Lagertha's beast, when it came to the trials involving Aslaug, he was much more forgiving. While he tried to persuade Aslaug to sleep with him, and to leave Spangareid, when Aslaug refused, he seemed to willingly oblige her requests.

The only time there seems to be some conflict in regard to Aslaug's trials is on their wedding night when Aslaug insists they wait three days before consummating the relationship. This does not happen and, as a result, Ivar is born a cripple. Even still, Ragnar shows none of the resentment present in Lagertha's story.

These trials between Ragnar and the significant women in his life were common in stories of the time. Many of the sagas tell of trials that must be performed before a marriage proposal is accepted. Once such famous instance of a saga trial involves King Harald Fairhair. In this example, Harald must become the king of all Norway before he can wed Gyda, the daughter of Eirik, the king of Hordaland.

After Ragnar and Aslaug wed, they become parents to some of the most famous Vikings of all. These sons would go on to do great things and conquer a multitude of places. So, it could be said that while Ragnar and Aslaug had a great love story within their saga, perhaps the best thing to come out of their union was their children.

Sigurd Snake-in-the-Eye has a daughter who will give birth to Harald Fairhair, the man mentioned previously who would go on to become the first united king of all Norway.

Many people are also claim they are descended from Bjorn Ironside. Considering he founded the great Munso clan, it is no surprise as to these claims. Besides this prestige, Bjorn also raided many places, going as far as the Mediterranean in his Viking pursuits.

While Ivar the Boneless might not have had any children, his story still lives on. It is said he ruled over a large proportion of England until his death. On his sickbed, as he lay dying, he asked he be buried in the place where raiders might come so his spirit might prevent those who planned to attack. When King Harald Sigurdarson reached that place, he fell because of Ivar's curse. But later, when William the Bastard landed, he tore down Ivar's burial mound. Discovering Ivar's body still-intact, he instructed for it to be burned, thus, breaking his curse.

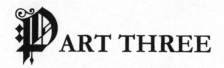

PART THREE

LOOKING FURTHER INTO THE WORLD OF
THE VIKINGS

REFERENCES

When one starts to delve into the history of the Vikings, it seems there are only a few major sources. However, myriad resources as well as various translations and scholarly tomes and articles delve into various stories involving the Vikings.

Therefore, this joint venture of a fiction and nonfiction account of Aslaug and Ragnar's romance has not been a simple one. Below is the list of resources I have used over the entirety of writing *Vikings: The Truth about Aslaug and Ragnar*. Many were used for direct research, whereas others were used as inspiration or to gather a greater understanding of the Viking Age. Feel free to peruse each resource as required in your search to uncover more truths behind the Vikings and their era.

Some of these texts, being so old, fall outside of copyright, so are freely accessible online. Many of these texts can also be found as scanned documents on archive.org or as reproduced documents on Project Gutenberg. Both sites offer various formats to either view or download each item.

Archive.org is an online resource where out of copyright books, documents, letters, video, etc. have been scanned, uploaded and, where required, digitalised, by Google so that people can access these resources easily.

Project Gutenberg is another online resource aiming to bring out of copyright tomes within the reach of everyone. If you prefer to use this resource, you can simply visit gutenberg.org and start searching.

Alcuin of York: His Life and Letters. Allott, S. (ed and trans). (York, 1974). letter no. 26, 36–8.

Historical Works of Simeon of Durham, The. Symeon of Durham, Stevenson, J. (translated) (1855). Church Historians of England, volume III, part II.

Icelandic Sagas. These sources are many and varied. The best place to start researching this source is probably the website, Icelandic Saga Database (http://www.sagadb.org/). It must be noted however, that not all of the sagas listed on this website are available in English.

Icelandic Sagas and Other Historical Documents Relating to the Settlements and Descents of the Northmen on the British Isles Vol III - The Orkneyinger's Saga. Rerum Britannicarum Medii Ævi Scriptores, Or, *Chronicles and Memorials of Great Britain and Ireland During the Middle Ages.* Dasent, G. (Great Britain. 1894). University of Minnesota. (Public Record Office).

Prose Edda, The. Sturluson, S., Gilchrist, A. (1916). Brodeur.

Poetic Edda, The. Bellows, H. (translated). (New York, 1923) The American-Scandinavian Foundation. As discussed earlier in the section on sources used, *The Poetic Edda* can be considered interchangeable with another source called the *Codex Regius.*

Nowell Codex. Cotton MS Vitellius A XV. Each component of the volume contained within the Nowell Codex was acquired by Sir Robert Bruce Cotton (b. 1571, d. 1631). This collection was expanded on by his son, Sir Thomas Cotton (b. 1594, d. 1662), and grandson, Sir John Cotton (b. 1621, d. 1702). The entire collection was then bequeathed to trustees "for Publick Use and Advantage." According to the British Library, who hold the original documents, the previous ownership of the respective parts is as follows:(i) [f 1]: made in England (ii) f 3: made in England (iii) ff 4–93: made in England; owned by Southwick Priory (Hampshire) (iv) ff 94–209: made in England; owned by Laurence Nowell (d. c. 1570).

Anglo Saxon Chronicle. Edited from the translation in *Monumenta Historica Britanica and Other Versions* by the Late J. A. Giles D C.L. New Edition. (1914). London G. Bell and Sons, Ltd.

Danish History, Book IX, The. Grammaticus, S., Elton, O. (translated). (1861-1945) & Powell, F. York (1850-1904).

Danish History Books I-X, The. Grammaticus, S. (2016). Perennial Press This edition includes the original copy of the *Gesta Danorum* from the version available free online at the Gutenberg Project that has been translated by Oliver Elton (Norroena Society, New York, 1905) and edited, proofed, and prepared by Douglas B. Killings.

Gods and Myths of Northern Europe. Ellis Davidson, H. (1964). Pelican Books.

Heimskringla: A History of the Norse Kings. Sturluson, S., Monsen, E. (translated), and Smith, A. (New York, 1932). Dover Publications, Inc.

Knútsrápra by Sigvatr Þórðarson, Skaldic Poetry of the Scandinavian Middle Ages.

Meeting the Other in Norse Myth in Legends. McKinnell, J. (2005). D.S. Brewer.

Norse Mythology. Gaiman, N. (Great Britain, 2017). Bloomsbury Publishing Plc.

Penguin Historical Atlas of the Vikings, The. Haywood, J. (1995). Swanston Publishing Limited.

Roles of the Northern Goddess. Davidson, H. (1998, 2002). Routledge.

Sagas of Ragnar Lodbrok, The, Waggoner, B. (Connecticut, 2009). The Troth.

Saxo Grammaticus: The History of the Danes, Books I-IX: I. English Text; II. Commentary (Bks.1-9). Fisher, P. (translated). (Cambridge, 1980). D. S. Brewer.

Scandinavian Mythology. Ellis Davidson, H. (United States, 1969). The Hamlyn Publishing Group Limited.

Symeonis Dunelmensis Opera et collectanea. Simeon of Durham. (1130) and, Hodgson-Hinde, J. (1868).

Viking atrocity and Skaldic verse: The Rite of the Blood-Eagle. Frank, R. (1984). Oxford University Press.

Women in Old Norse Society. Jochens, J. (1995). Cornell

University Press.

If you enjoyed this book, please consider leaving a review on Amazon and Goodreads. A long review is not needed, just by adding a short sentence or two helps other potential readers find this book.

ℬOOKS BY RACHEL TSOUMBAKOS

Historical Fiction/Fantasy
Ragnar and the Women Who Loved Him (Viking Secrets #0)
Vikings: The Truth about Lagertha and Ragnar (Viking Secrets #1)
Vikings: The Truth about Thora and Ragnar (Viking Secrets #2)
Vikings: The Trouble with Ubbe's Mother (Viking Secrets #3)
Vikings: The Truth about Aslaug and Ragnar (Viking Secrets #4)
The Unnamed Warrior (Valkyrie Secrets #1)
Curse of the Valkyries (Valkyrie Secrets #2)
The Breaker of Curses (Valkyrie Secrets #3)
The Lost Viking (short story set in the same universe of Viking Secrets and Valkyrie Secrets)

Paranormal
Emeline and the Mutants
The Ring of Lost Souls
Metanoia
Unremembered Things

Horror
Zombie Apocalypse Now!

Make sure you sign up for my newsletter to find out when the next book in this series is due for release. You can do so here: bit.ly/RachelNL

Index

Made in the USA
Las Vegas, NV
02 April 2021

20639546R00152